WITCHES
&
VAMPIRES

Vampire
Encampment

Sunlight Hallow

Palladium Forest

The
Underground

Rebel Camp

Dark
Shadows
Headquarters

Meadow Ville

WITCHES & VAMPIRES

BRIANNA WITTE

atmosphere press

To my family. Thank you for believing in me and helping my dreams become a reality.

CHAPTER 1

Merissa

A gust of wind blew my smooth, light-brown hair into the air, making it dance in the spring breeze. The noisy buzz of broomsticks flying up into the bright, blue sky echoed in my ears. The smell of the freshly baked pastries floated into my nose as I walked past the bakeries lining the cobblestone streets.

A child smashed into my arm as he ran past me, filling the street with giggles and laughter while his sister chased him.

"Sorry," he yelled as he darted through the crowd of wizards walking around the bustling town.

Rubbing my sore arm, I turned around watching as a tall, slender woman crouched down and opened her arms toward the small siblings. The children ran into their mother's loving embrace, smiling before pulling her into one of the sweets shops nearby.

I couldn't help but envy those children. They had the one thing I could never have: A permanent home with caring parents that would never abandon them.

Although my aunt and uncle had done a miraculous job of raising me and I loved them dearly, I still couldn't shake the feeling of being alone. My parents had disappeared not long after I was born, leaving me to be raised by my Aunt Lucy and Uncle Ashtyn.

I shouldn't complain. They treated me like I was their own daughter. In fact, I always thought they were my birth parents, until one day they decided to tell me the truth. They figured I was old enough to comprehend and handle my adoption. However, my curiosity and desire to learn more about the people who bore me only gave way to an endless fixation.

I had wanted to know everything about them. What they looked like. How they met and, most importantly, how they disappeared.

For a good chunk of my youth, I would try to pry the answers out of my aunt and uncle but, they wouldn't budge. They said I was too young to learn what had happened, that I was safer if I knew nothing about them.

The constant relocating to various towns and cities made me wonder if my parents had done something terrible. Uncle Ashtyn only accepted temporary jobs, causing us to move from town-to-town; from school-to-school. I was never in one place for more than a year.

This intensified my loneliness. I didn't have enough time to make real friends, and Aunt Lucy was always supervising me, making sure that nothing bad could happen. After losing her brother and sister-in-law, I knew she had every right to be defensive of their only daughter.

Being protective of your child is only natural, but my aunt and uncle seemed to cling to me like I was constantly about to make a fatal leap from a cliff. They were always with me, never letting me out of their sight.

Aunt Lucy and Uncle Ashtyn had been overprotective of me since the beginning of my life. I needed my own freedom.

Now that I was sixteen, they had given me some space; I was at an age where I wasn't as vulnerable. I was able to roam unsupervised, no more bodyguards in sight.

On my way back home, I followed the same route as I had since we moved to Sunlight Hollow. I made a routine out of it, although my aunt and uncle forbade me to do so. It made me feel like I had more control over my life. I was able to make my own decisions, have the freedom I craved, as any teenager would. No longer did I have to follow my aunt and uncle's rules. I was my own person.

I stuffed my cold hands into the pockets of my jeans to keep them warm. They pressed against my thighs, sending shivers down my legs.

I looked into a shop window, staring at the beautifully embroidered clothing inside. In the reflection, I could see the shapes of houses sitting high on the mountain behind me; their massive stone exterior highlighted in the midday sun. Many people strive to live in those kinds of homes, their gated properties and stone exterior creating the impression of wealth.

I couldn't care less about a property like that. I prefer the smaller homes at the bottom of the mountain. Their simple complexion and wooden frames made it feel cozy and family oriented, not something to gloat about.

Looking out at the mountainous range behind me made me realize just how small and remote Sunlight Hollow was in the country of Elontra.

Compared to some of the other towns we had moved to, Sunlight Hollow was situated in a wealthy, isolated community; a place filled with vacation homes and retirement living. The mountains gave a great view of Elontra's vast landscape and the town sat close to the sea.

I turned away from the shop window, looking around me at all of the witches and wizards chatting away as they roamed the streets.

Being a remote area, Sunlight Hollow was a full wizarding community. It was very rare to find another species in town. Wizards took over the majority of the planet of Syrine; showing their dominance with sheer numbers. From my experience, the other creatures that inhabited Syrine were found mainly in cities, where they stayed together in the same neighborhoods for comfort.

The large clock in the town square sounded, sending its loud chime echoing throughout the town.

It was time to head home for lunch. Aunt Lucy would get worried if I didn't return for her famous grilled chicken wraps.

As I looked back to see the dazzling ocean through two large trees, I noticed two people in hooded black capes farther behind me. Even with the streets crowded with shoppers, they were noticeable from a distance.

My heart fluttered in my chest. Throughout the planet of Syrine, no one wore the colour black. It was a symbol of dark magic; a magic so forbidden that it was completely banned in Elontra. I quickly turned down another street and began to walk at a faster pace. My gut screamed that something wasn't right; that something bad was about to take place.

I glanced back again to see the same hooded figures following me down the street, increasing their pace to match mine.

Screams echoed in the streets. The crowd took notice and frantically ran to keep their distance. The streets cleared out faster than I could possibly imagine and the sound of doors locking made me want to cry. I had nowhere to hide.

I began to shake as I dashed onto yet another street and began to run. I pushed my hair out of my face to see where the hooded figures were. My heart nearly ceased when I only saw one hooded person right behind me. Where had the other gone?

Suddenly the feeling of a cold, invisible chain grabbed my leg, making me fall to the ground. It quickly dragged me into a dark alley. I let out a scream as I dug my nails into the cobblestone alleyway, trying to keep whatever magic this was from taking me any further.

The invisible chain continued to drag me into the alley until I saw the second person. They held a wand and chanted something that I couldn't understand. The hooded figure dropped down and held me on the ground, pinning me while their friend caught up.

I screamed for help one last time before one of the hooded figures clasped their rough hands over my mouth. I couldn't tell which one was which anymore. Adrenaline coursed through my veins. The only thing I could think of doing was getting out of this situation alive.

I kicked, hit, scratched and did whatever I could to make them let go. Pain shot through my body as they swiftly turned me around, pulled my arms behind my back and smashed me against the pavement in order to keep me under control.

An explosion of pain spread through my head as it hit the cold, hard ground. My eyes closed. The sound of the village faded into nothing. Then everything went black.

. . .

I awoke in a panic, remembering every event that occurred before I had passed out. I felt warm, cotton blankets wrapped around my body. I was lying on a bed staring at the ceiling.

I turned my head to find that I was in a luxurious bedroom.

The room was a deep, red color and had hardwood floors. A white bed and a matching dresser were opposite of each other against the walls. A door was left wide open for me to see that it led to a washroom. The bedroom had a large closet with sliding doors and two stunning paintings hung on each side of a huge window, overlooking a beautiful forest on the mountainous hillside.

Where was I?

I jolted upright, checking my pockets for my wand. I let out a fearful gasp. My wand was missing; my only way of defense gone. My chest rapidly moved up and down as I flew into a panic.

I rushed to the casement windows, pulling at the elegant metal handles. I tugged as hard as I could but they didn't move. I slammed my hands on the glass as tears swelled in my eyes.

Looking out into the distance, there was no help in sight. A large property spread before me; the tall trees and extravagant gardens making it seem as if it would go on forever.

Suddenly, a sharp pain spread through my head. I pressed my hands against my temple as I curled up into a ball, feeling powerless.

No. I couldn't break down now. I had to get out of here, away from whoever had taken me. If my initial instinct was true and they were using dark magic, I was in terrible danger. Panic only leads to death. If I wanted to survive, I needed to think before acting.

I slowly lifted my head looking for a way out. There was only one door on the opposite side of the room. I rushed over to it as quickly as possible without making too much noise.

I turned the knob and, of course, it was locked. I leaned against the door as dread swept through me. I should have listened to my Aunt and Uncle's rules. I should never have made a routine. These people were obviously following me, knowing I was an easy target.

Frustration clawed at me until it was oozing out of my pores. I was ready to explode into tears. I twisted the knob hard trying to force it to move. Open, darn it, open, my mind shrieked as I pushed at the door with determination.

Suddenly I felt a rush of energy blast out of me, aiming at the door. I stared at the knob in a trance until the lock clicked. The energy that I felt vanished, leaving a sense of calm washing over me. I had felt this before. It was what I called casting.

Most witches needed their wands to use their magic. I found that when I become emotional I don't. The first time it happened I told my aunt. Following her startled reaction, she declared that I was never to tell anyone else or try casting again. But I couldn't control it at times. Was this why the hooded figures took me? I shook my head, forcing out all the questions I had; knowing my only focus now was getting out of this place.

I turned my shaking hand and the knob followed along with it. I let out a deep breath and silently pulled the door all the way open. My legs shook as I crept down each step of a long wooden staircase. My heart raced in my chest. I didn't want to face those hooded figures again, but I knew that if I couldn't find my way out, I wouldn't stand a chance.

As I stopped silently on the last step, I peeked around the corner of the wall.

I heard two voices mumbling somewhere in a kitchen. I leaned towards the voices to try and hear what that they were saying. I thought I heard someone say my name but I couldn't be sure.

I stepped off the stairs and onto the hardwood floor keeping my back pinned against the wall.

Another set of mumbled words echoed in the kitchen before I heard footsteps coming towards me. Before I could react, a blond haired woman appeared looking straight at me. Every inch of heat in my body was replaced by a cold, icy feeling. We both froze. The woman stared at me; her mouth open in shock.

"Evelyn!" called the woman.

As soon as she spoke another woman with long, black hair darted out of the kitchen. She gasped as she laid her deep green eyes on me.

"Emma grab her!" shrieked Evelyn.

My muscles screamed for me to run and I obeyed. I spun around and dashed to the door, but the women caught up to me quicker than I figured. Evelyn grabbed me from behind and spun us both around so I was facing Emma once more. She pushed me towards the living room.

I struggled to free myself from Evelyn's grasp in any way that I could. She called out for help. While doing so one of my arms slipped out from her grip. I violently swung my arm up until I felt my elbow make contact with bone. Evelyn threw me away from her, clutching her nose as a stream of blood ran down from it.

I ran for the door and swung it open. A wave of relief hit me as my feet touched the stone porch. I ran as fast as I could, but my heart nearly stopped once I saw that I had to get through a high metal gate to get off of the property. I smashed into the gate and struggled to open it, but it was locked.

I glanced up and realized that I could climb it. The drop shouldn't hurt me too badly.

I gripped the white, metal bars of the gate tightly as I scrambled up, trying desperately not to slip or fall. I felt tugging at my legs. My feet slipped off the metal but I used all the muscle in my arms to pull me back up. Once I regained my balance, I looked down to see that the women had caught up with me. Emma's feet were perched on the lower bars as she reached for me.

I tried to climb higher but Emma caught up to me. Her arms wrapped around my waist and pulled me back down to the ground where Evelyn waited holding a bloody cloth to her nose.

Both women dragged me back into the house ignoring my screams for help. Evelyn yanked me up the stairs while Emma blocked my only exit. I was thrust back into the same bedroom that I previously occupied. Emma held me down on the bed.

"You can scream and run all you want but no one will help you."

"You're wrong!" I yelled back.

"No Merissa. No one knows where you are and they never will."

My heart sank into my chest leaving a feeling of hopelessness. My muscles slacked as defeat consumed me.

"Why are you doing this to me?" I cried.

"It's our job," said Emma.

Evelyn's enraged gaze turned to Emma.

"Emma, don't say anymore. She doesn't need to know. Make sure the lock is sealed this time. Do you understand me?" said Evelyn as she walked out of the room.

Emma nodded obediently as she slowly released me. I laid on the bed motionless. The door shut and the sound of a key turning in the lock made me feel sick.

With today's events racing through my mind, I tried to piece together the intentions of these women. I could hear an argument brewing downstairs. I listened to the women as their voices grew louder and louder.

"Why did you have to tell her that? I thought we agreed that she shouldn't know anything?!" Evelyn shrieked.

"I did not reveal any important information and we both know she needs to lose hope of escaping. It's the only way we can control her. Now that she knows there's no way to flee, we won't have to watch her every second!"

"Really, you think that will stop her! She's going to try again, and when she succeeds, we'll be the ones punished, just like what happened when she was a baby!" said Evelyn with a hint of fear in her voice.

"She won't succeed, and this will not be the same situation we faced before. No one will find her and return her to safety again."

"You can't be sure about that. She's old enough to make her own decisions and those decisions could be our undoing. If we lose her again..."

Denial swept though me like a massive wave washing up on shore. This couldn't be possible. They must have the wrong person.

No. They were talking specifically about me. What did they want with me?

Dizziness washed over me and my head felt like it was about to explode. A sudden wave of light headedness hit me and then everything around me went dark.

. . .

I opened my eyes and realized that I was still on the bed. I had no idea how long I had been passed out. I looked out the window and saw the sun still high in the sky. It couldn't have been very long.

I felt like I was being watched. I turned my head to see Emma leaning over me in fear.

"Are you all right, Merissa? What happened?"

Anger exploded inside me once I saw Emma. I couldn't believe she did this to me. Both women took away everything I had but for what purpose?

Instead of lashing out, I pushed these feelings down. It wouldn't help me right now.

"Maybe the bump on her head was worse than we thought. You should let her rest," said a man's voice.

My head jerked toward the door to see a man with short, brown hair and deep, green eyes.

"Maybe, I'm not sure. She seemed all right beforehand...but I do agree she should get rest. I had a feeling her injury might be worse than it seemed," said Evelyn, who'd stopped her bleeding nose and cleaned her face.

I felt weak from whatever just happened but didn't let it show, knowing that they could take advantage of it.

After making sure I was alright, Evelyn and the man left the room. Before Emma could leave, I grabbed her hand and she quickly turned around.

"Who was that?" I asked.

Emma stared at me, emotionless. She pulled her hand away from me. She followed Evelyn, slamming the door behind her before turning the lock, leaving me once again imprisoned in the room.

CHAPTER 2

Derik

Syrine may be filled with a variety of different magical beings, but that doesn't mean that we are all seen as equal. Wizards dominated the planet, leaving every other race a minority. Some were driven away onto secluded continents for being deemed too dangerous and unpredictable, such as the werewolves for having a taste for wizard's blood once their monthly change had begun. Others were welcome to live among the wizards, as they were no threat.

Vampires had been seen as the lowest class on the planet for centuries. Although the Dark Shadows were the main cause of this stereotype, I believe it began long before they rose to power. We were thought of as dirty and dangerous because of our strict diet of blood. We were looked down upon, looked as something to stay away from, rather than to befriend.

Once the Dark Shadows figured out that vampires were of valuable use to maintaining their power, they began enslaving us. Our stereotype became even more prominent. Those who were captured lived a life of poverty and cruel treatment. There were very few ways to rebel against the Dark Shadows. They were too powerful and had most vampires kneeling before them in fear of being killed.

Those who remained free didn't live a much better life. They lived in the Underground, a massive, dark, submersive cave, which was a whole world inside of the planet of Syrine. It was a heavily populated vampire city that provided refuge from the Dark Shadows.

Although we were safely hidden away, the conditions

of the city had withered with time. Some of the candle lit lanterns that were the only source of light, needed to be replaced because of the loss of material. Buildings that were once made out of fresh wood and stable brick had begun to deteriorate. Blood supplies had become limited since most living creatures inside the Underground's lush gardens were becoming extinct. Scouts were trained to go above ground and bring back supplies to maintain the city. However, it was a dangerous task, and some were never seen again, either taken by the Dark Shadows or presumed dead.

We were taught about what life was like aboveground; how the sun would heat your skin. Fresh, cold water took up large portions of land, unlike our underground lake that was our only source of drinkable water. The scouts would come back with stories about the clean air and the massive trees. I only wished I could live aboveground, but the Dark Shadows made that next to impossible.

The Underground was my home. The home I no longer wanted to stay in.

. . .

"I signed up to be a scout again. I was turned down for the second time," I said.

My mother's delicate brown eyes widened in fear as she rapidly turned to face me, sending her black curls flying in the air.

"Derik! I've told you this before. You're only seventeen and are far too young to go aboveground. I don't want you to become one of the many missing scouts."

"Well, I don't want to waste the rest of my life living in

a rotting city and become unable to adjust to the sunlight. I want to have my own life and I don't want to be like everyone else. I..."

"That's enough of this nonsense! I won't lose you like I lost your father! This conversation is over!" my mother said as she scrambled out of the lounging area.

Just mentioning my father's death raised my hackles. He was one of the best scouts until the Dark Shadows tried to recruit him as a spy in the Underground; offering freedom and power in their ranks. When my father turned them down, he was tortured until he died a bloody and painful death.

I won't end up like him. He taught me every skill he knew until I perfected it. I will live a better life and avenge my father. His death will not be in vain.

. . .

The next morning, I left without saying goodbye. It would have been too hard to leave my mother if I had.

I didn't look back as I ran out of the city and climbed up the steep slopes that led to an emergency exit. A tall, old, rickety ladder laid against the rough cave wall. I carefully climbed it until a small, thick metal plate came into focus. I pushed up the plate, which was heavy enough so no one other than a vampire could lift, and found myself in a forest.

As I climbed out of the hole and into a forest, I put the plate back into place and covered it back up with dirt. Happiness radiated off of me. I could smell fresh air and feel the light morning breeze against my pale skin for the first time in my life.

Most wizards think that vampires are the living dead; that we can't survive in sunlight and live for an eternity as monsters lingering in the shadows. But those are only myths created from being forced underground. We are not immortal; we age and die just the same as anyone else. We can survive in the sunlight, but with time we can lose our ability to adjust to it; we become nocturnal. Vampires are the same as wizards. The only difference is that our main diet is blood, and instead of magic, we have enhanced abilities to help us hunt down prey. We are stronger and faster than most other beings, making us able to catch almost anything; even creatures twice our size.

I brushed dirt off my plain, grey tank top and jeans. A sharp gust of wind nearly toppled me over.

I stuck my nose in the air and took a deep breath. The musk of moist dirt clouded my nostrils. I stared up, smiling at the clear, blue sky. The giant, fiery sun shone down on me, allowing me to feel its glorious heat. For the first time in my life, I felt completely free.

I walked briskly further into the forest, my hands feeling the delicate leaves on the trees and the fresh air through my fingers. I shouted out in joy as I jumped into a river, splashing in the cool water before crossing it.

With my clothes dripping wet, I followed what appeared to be a trail.

Unexpectedly, I heard twigs crack behind me. I spun around to see the outline of a body in the shadows.

The feeling of happiness ceased as my senses went into overdrive. I took a deep breath in the direction of the intruder and the scent of a vampire caught my attention. Could it be a scout?

The figure walked into a patch of light, allowing me to

see his tattered clothes and matted hair. I knew everyone in the Underground, this was a complete stranger. To me, he looked like he had been aboveground for a long time; his skin tanned compared to mine which was ghostly white. At that moment I saw the unmistakable trademark of a captured vampire: the black band of magic, looking like streaks of lightning encircling his wrist, glowed against the vampire's clothing. We were warned about this mark. It meant you were forever enslaved by the Dark Shadows; someone who was owned. They placed the band on your wrist as a tracker. There was no escape once it was on. Only a wizard could remove it and it was highly unlikely anyone would mess with the Dark Shadows.

The figure started to move toward me. I turned and ran in the opposite direction as fast as I could. I could hear the vampire following me. Two more sets of footsteps joined in. He wasn't alone.

My heart pounded as I darted into a town ahead of me but, to my surprise it looked empty. The streets were bare. Every building had boarded up windows and broken doors. Weeds sprouted up out of the cobblestone as if no one had stepped foot on them in years.

Around the town, tall trees and mountainous terrain spread for miles. A sinking feeling seeped into my gut. There was no escape in sight; only pure wilderness.

I took another deep breath. This broken settlement reeked of vampires.

I've heard stories of these types of towns. The Dark Shadows seal off certain areas used to house vampire slaves. I'd been led right into one.

Panic erupted inside me. The vampires weren't chasing me at random. This was planned. They were waiting for a young, foolish vampire to come out of hiding. They knew where we were. Instead of wasting resources to begin an attack, they were waiting for us to come to them. This was an ambush.

I heard their footsteps casually approach me as they blocked the nearest exits.

I could see all of the vampire's faces now. Dirt caked on their skin. Tattered clothes hung off their muscular frames. Matted hair touched their shoulders. The worse sight was their eyes tinted red, a sign that they had drunk directly from a wizard's magic-filled veins not too long ago.

I was told the horror stories of how some vampires approved of the Dark Shadows ways; that instead of being a slave, they thought of themselves as followers.

I could see the ambition in all three of the vampire's eyes. I got the sense they enjoyed evoking pain upon others, even their own kind. The pleasure they gained from my fear made them smile a cruel grin.

Although I was scared stiff, I straightened my back, clenched my fists, bared my fangs and braced for a fight.

The three vampires began to move towards me in an aggressive manner. One of them let out an arrogant laugh; his eyes displaying his desire for blood lust. Suddenly, the vampires stopped. Footsteps echoed behind me.

"That's enough. I'll take him from here," said the vampire.

I swiftly turned around to see another vampire with fearsome, dark-blue eyes and long, blond hair standing right behind me. Reluctantly the three vampires sulked away just like a wolf obeying its pack leader.

"Come with me," the vampire said turning to me.

"Why should I?"

"Where else are you going to go? We are noticeable around here and the Dark Shadows will be able to find you easily," said the vampire as he began to walk back to where he came from.

I hesitated before following. I could get a head start and run right now. I would be free. But he was right. There was no place to go. I was an outsider and would only stand out aboveground. I couldn't go home either. The Dark Shadows would only follow me. Our safe haven was now a ticking time bomb waiting to explode. Eventually, the Dark Shadows would come for the Underground and destroy all that I ever knew.

If I ever wanted to get my revenge, I needed to play along and find the right opportunity to strike.

As we went deeper into the heart of the town, more vampires surrounded me, but the conditions of the town didn't improve. Vampires stared at me, some in pity and others in interest.

"What's your name?" I asked while trying to distract myself from the anxiety welling up inside me.

"Brock. Yours?"

"Derik."

"Well Derik, I'm in charge of newcomers. I'll show you where you'll be staying before giving you the ground rules..." said Brock.

Suddenly a loud, frantic voice rang throughout the small town.

"Please don't hurt me! I didn't mean to do anything wrong!" a man cried.

I strode around a building to see a wizard with his arm outstretched holding his wand. The three vampires I encountered earlier surrounded a man who knelt on the hard dirt ground with tears streaming out of his eyes.

"You were caught smuggling out vampires from our encampment. Now you must face the wrath of the Dark Shadows. What do you three think we should do with him?" asked the wizard.

"You should let me drain his blood. I would enjoy another snack before I get back to work," said one of the vampires, licking his thin dry lips.

Blind rage coursed through my veins. They were going to hurt an innocent man trying to do some good in the world. I bolted toward the wizard, striking him in the face with my fist. The blow knocked him to the ground in shock as blood rushed out of his nose.

The crying man took this opportunity to rush out of sight. The three vampires dashed after him, leaving the wizard on the ground to fend for himself.

Before I could do any more damage, the wizard quickly got to his feet and raised his wand to my heart.

"Justin, don't kill him! He's new! He'll learn obedience," shouted Brock as he jumped between Justin and me.

Justin turned his attention back to me with his wand still raised.

"So this is the new vampire I was just informed about...I'll let you off with a warning," the wizard, Justin, said.

His wand came down upon my wrist so fast that I didn't have time to react. A jolt of electricity wrapped around my wrist sending pain shooting up my arm. I cried out in anguish as my skin burned and throbbed. I held back my tears as the slave band appeared upon my wrist, the black lightning streaks crackling in my ears and the smell of burnt flesh clogging my nostrils.

"You better make sure you don't interfere with my business for a second time or, I swear, you won't see daylight ever again. I will not allow disobedience in my ranks."

Justin turned to Brock saying in a voice of contempt, "Since you were brave enough to stand up for him, you will take full responsibility for this vampire's actions. If anything else happens it will be on your head." Then, he vanished into the shadows of one of the many dark alleys.

. . .

Brock and I walked up a steep, wooden staircase on an old rickety building in silence. I could tell by the unpleasant look on his face and his clenched fists that he was less than happy with the situation.

As we reached the fourth level, I followed Brock through a set of cracked wooden doors and into a narrow hallway. The floor squeaked under my feet. The dull wallpaper was ripping apart, leaving the wooden wall bare.

"Who's this?" asked a young vampire leaning against the wall in front of one of the rooms.

"Kevin, this is Derik. He was just brought in. He'll be across the hall from you so keep an eye on him while he gets accustomed to his new life here," said Brock, looking at me with a hint of rage in his eyes.

Brock opened a door directly across from Kevin and ordered me inside. He slammed the door shut as soon as I crossed the threshold. His large hands grabbed the front on my shirt and threw me against the wall.

"Never do that again. You serve the Dark Shadows now. The only thing you should be worried about is your life, which is something that they do not care about," he whispered in my ear angrily.

"I'm in charge of you and if you mess up, then I get punished as well. The advice I have for you is to keep your head low and follow orders. Don't be a hero."

Brock let go of me, slamming the door open as he left the room.

I stood against the wall, shaken.

"What did you do to get him so upset?" Kevin laughed.

"Who's Justin? What's his role with the Dark Shadows?" I asked, panicked.

"Justin is one of the highest members of the Dark Shadows. He's the one that's in charge of all the vampires. His job is to keep us under control and give us orders. Was he the one who gave you the slave band? How do you know about him?"

I ignored Kevin's question as fear rose inside of me. I just got on the bad side of an important and well-known Dark Shadow member.

CHAPTER 3

Merissa

That evening Emma and the man, whom I heard being called Richard, left without explanation. I was alone with Evelyn, leaving her unaided and me with an advantage.

If Emma and Evelyn thought I would simply cower in a corner when things got tough, then they were wrong. I was not a scared little girl. Regardless of what they did to me or how many times I was recaptured, I would escape. It would only be a matter of time before I succeeded.

I heard Evelyn's footsteps come up the stairs. I quietly stepped closer to the door, waiting for it to unlock. The lock clicked and the door slowly creaked open. This was my only opportunity. I ran at Evelyn landing my fist into her soft stomach. Her eyes grew wide as she leaned down and clutched her abdomen, gasping for breath.

My heart pounded as I dashed downstairs to the main floor.

I ran toward the back of the house, hoping I'd have somewhere to go. Just as I managed to get to the kitchen, Evelyn caught up to me, pointing her wand in my direction. A spell hit a vase of roses with such force that it exploded into pieces around me. Evelyn fired again, but I ducked behind a counter in fear. I gasped as the spell went flying past my head and hit a glass vase on the counter.

I could hear Evelyn walking across the broken glass as she approached my hiding spot. Every step made a shiver crawl up my spine. She was so close now that I could hear her uneven breaths clearly. Her shoes came into view and our eyes met for a split second.

Before Evelyn could react, I kicked her legs out from beneath her. She fell to the floor in pain. I ran as if my life depended on it, trying to make it to the door.

I didn't get far before I stumbled and fell on a piece of glass from the decoration Evelyn's spell had smashed.

Evelyn pivoted on the ground and swung her wand toward me again. It was all over in a flash. A sedation spell hit me square in the chest, making me gasp before my eyes drew shut.

Emma

"Are you ready to go in?" asked the vampire.

"Open the doors," I said firmly.

The vampire held open the bulky, wooden doors of the refined, upscale townhouse. My stomach turned as I entered one of the many secret locations the Dark Shadows used in the wealthy neighborhood of Sunlight Hollow.

I took a deep breath, trying to calm my shaky hands before this meeting began. Since Merissa's capture, my husband, Richard, and I have had to keep up our appearances even more.

Playing the part of a loyal Dark Shadow was harder than I could have possibly imagined. Watching innocent people suffer by my own hand has given me nightmares that shake me to my core. What made things even harder was knowing that the Dark Shadows had finally recaptured my loving niece and indeed had plans for her demise.

If it weren't for Merissa, Richard and I would have kept ourselves far away from the Dark Shadows. They were a ruthless pack of wild animals, striving to acquire power through whatever means necessary.

It was hard watching my sister and her husband being locked away in a dungeon for almost two decades and their daughter placed on the run. Through all of these years I still couldn't help but feel that I had betrayed them, although my intentions were the exact opposite.

Yet, Richard and I were the only ones that could save Merissa. We had helped her escape the Dark Shadows before; using the opportunity of a rebellion to sneak baby Merissa to Lucy and Ashtyn.

It had taken a long time to earn back the Dark Shadow's trust, but I'm sure by now we have enough of it to free Merissa again.

Whether I must sacrifice this charade or my life, I will not let them harm my niece.

I climbed down the stairs to a basement where Evelyn's husband, Justin, and an elderly witch named Cora were standing around a cauldron waiting for me.

Cora could be described as the Dark Shadows' potion master; a chemist. All you needed to do was name the potion that you desired and she would create it to your ideals.

"...I will not let that young, naive vampire spread rebellion throughout my town. He stands for everything I worked so hard to bring down," said Justin angrily.

"Don't worry, Justin. They all come around at some point. You just need to show him who's in charge; make him fear you."

Cora turned to me, looking at me impatiently as if I had arrived hours late.

"Now that we're all here, let's get to work. Hand me the vial Justin."

Justin took out a small glass vial labeled '*Merissa's*

blood'. He carefully pulled the cork out of the top of the vial and poured the thick, red liquid into the cauldron.

The steaming hot water slowly turned into the thick, metallic smelling blood. Large amounts of gold flakes glittered in the cauldron, showing the huge amount of magic inside Merissa.

"Oh...she is indeed powerful," Cora watched the cauldron as if expecting something to happen.

"Now that we have a sample of Merissa's powers, we can test how to extract them from her. I have a feeling that the potion I would normally prepare will not work effectively on her."

"How long will it take?" I asked.

"As I have learned with my previous experience, extracting magic from someone is extremely difficult. It can take an awfully long time to figure out how to remove it properly."

I let out a small sigh of relief. I may have some time to figure out how to free Merissa.

"Is it possible that she could die during the extraction?" I asked.

"There's certainly a possibility of Merissa dying in the process but all that really matters to us is removing the magic safely. The girl doesn't matter. She's merely a vessel."

My stomach turned, making bile rise in my throat. My deepest fears were coming true. If we fail to free Merissa, she will be killed. The Dark Shadows would have no more use for her. I must let Richard know. It was now a matter of life and death.

Merissa

I was stuck in the bedroom, yet again. I paced back and forth, unable to sit still. I was so close to escaping. Anger surged through my veins. I picked up a pillow and hurled it at the open closet, dislodging a wooden box and sending it crashing to the floor.

I jumped back in shock. How had that gotten there? I've searched every inch of this bedroom and never came across this.

I slowly walked up to the wooden box. My eyes grew wide and my entire body froze when I saw my name engraved in the top. I slowly knelt down and carefully opened the box. Despite my trembling hands I lifted out a beautiful, slick, wooden wand from inside.

My heart started pounding in my chest as I picked up a small note on the bottom of the box. It read, *'To our darling daughter Merissa. Love Mom and Dad'.*

Tears filled my eyes as I put the note gently back in the box and carefully studied the wand. This was something my parents had planned to give to me.

My eye caught sight of a small book in the same location that the box had fallen from. It was another item that had miraculously appeared out of nowhere. Realizing that it was a spell book, excitement radiated off me as I pulled it off the shelf. With my wand and the book combined, I could figure out how to break out of this horrible place.

I skimmed through the book, finding so many interesting things that I could use to my benefit. One particular spell caught my eye.

I read, *'The spell, Blindlight, is primarily used to distract an opponent with short rays of magical light. It blinds your opponent for only a few moments, but is found to be a useful opportunity to gain an advantage in battle.'*

I turned the next page and froze abruptly as I read the introduction to the final chapter.

'Curses and Dark Magic: Curses, whom many wizards believe to be a part of dark magic, are different and more dangerous from any other spells. Curses are the only magic that cause pain, or in extreme cases, death.'

I snapped my head away from the book as I heard the front door opening. Richard and Evelyn greeted Emma. I scrambled to hide the book as a pair of footsteps ascended the stairs. I shoved the book and wand under a bunch of clothes in the closet and jumped onto the bed just before Emma came into the room.

She stared at me suspiciously before locking the door again. It was just a checkup, I assured myself. I waited a few moments to make sure she was gone before I began to reach for the spell book again.

Just as I grabbed the book, a blinding bright light exploded into the room. As the light began to gradually fade, I saw a shadow of a small being floating in front of me. Delicate wings began to slowly emerge from the shadow. Small strands of vibrant red hair came down to the woman's shoulders in curly waves.

I was standing in the presence of a fairy.

CHAPTER 4

Derik

As I peered out of the window of my new residence, I couldn't help but notice tons of Dark Shadows roaming the streets and ordering vampires around. My stomach tightened in fear when one came closer to the building. Could this have something to do with my encounter with Justin yesterday?

All night, I had been paranoid. Having upset the ruler of the Dark Shadow's vampires, my vision of justice could easily be stopped before it had even begun.

The sound of my door opening startled me. I quickly swung my body around to face the intruder, but relaxed when I realized that it was Kevin.

"A little high strung aren't you," he called as he closed the door.

I turned my attention back to the window as I asked, "What's going on out there?"

"The Dark Shadows are taking those vampires away from their usual tasks. Two high-valued prisoners escaped from one of their dungeons the other day. Anyway, I came to get you because the Dark Shadows are recruiting us for a special assignment. They're waiting for us right now."

. . .

I followed Kevin, despite the bad feeling growing inside me, into an isolated part of the town where a group of vampires, including Brock, awaited us. As I got closer to the group, my body seemed tense all over. Standing amongst the vampires was Justin. His icy gaze followed me as I mingled with the group. This must be a mistake.

"Since we're all here, let's get started," said Justin with a harsh tone to his voice.

My heart pounded rapidly in my chest. This wasn't right. I should not have been recruited for a special assignment, especially if Justin was leading it.

"Most of you have heard rumors that we have come upon a being with immense powers," Justin continued, "This is no rumor. All of you have been selected for the task in aiding us in this situation. Most of you will be escorted to our headquarters where you will assist the Dark Shadows when we transport her there. The rest of you will stay here and remain at your usual posts until you're called upon to deal directly with this powerful witch..."

The rest of Justin's speech seemed to slowly fade out while only my own thoughts remained. There's a legend in the Underground about an extremely powerful witch that could defeat the Dark Shadows. I only thought it was a story; a fairytale told to give young vampires hope. But if it is true and Dark Shadows have her, they will be unstoppable.

"But I must warn you," I zoned back in to see Justin looking directly at me, "that with either assignment there is danger. Merissa is considered a risk. Yet this task is extremely important to the Dark Shadows. I advise you to not turn us into an even greater threat if you dare to defy the Dark Shadows at this sensitive point in time."

Fear clawed its way through my body. This wasn't a mistake. I was another roadblock on his way to power that needed to be destroyed. Justin chose me specifically because he wants me to fail.

. . .

After the meeting, Brock and I headed back into the centre of the town. Kevin stayed to be transported to the Dark Shadows headquarters, though something didn't seem right about him. The rest of the vampires stood rigid, scared of what was to come. Kevin stayed close to Justin, his body calm and a sense of happiness in his eyes. He was eager to prove himself to the Dark Shadows, as if he believed himself to be more of an ally than a slave.

I expected to get the duty of dealing directly with the witch. It seemed to be the most important task that would result in catastrophic consequences if neglected. After my previous encounter with Justin, he was indeed trying to get rid of me. He gave me the most important job so that I would not succeed and he had a reason to punish me.

As we walked, the shock of realizing Justin's true intent for me wore off. I realized this might be the best situation for me. This was a good opportunity to prevent the Dark Shadows from using Merissa to their advantage. Even if it means death, I would rather lose my life than stay a slave to them. Surprise flashed inside of me as I realized that I sounded just like my father before he died.

"Derik...," Brock whispered, "you need to be careful."

I faced Brock who had a look of alarm on his face.

"After what happened the other day, Justin wouldn't have personally selected us for this task. He must be trying to dispose of both of us. You need to watch your back and don't do anything stupid; think before you act. You're not the only one who will be killed if anything goes wrong."

A part of me wanted to listen to Brock, but the other part of me was too much like my father to care. I had to do something before it was too late.

If Merissa was as powerful as everyone believes, then she may be the key to ridding the world of the Dark Shadows. Together, we can end their reign once and for all.

CHAPTER 5

Merissa

I slowly backed away from the fairy floating in front of me. The fact that I was locked away in a secure area with no help in sight made me wonder if this creature was with the people who had captured me.

The fairy, noticing my actions, retreated to the opposite side of the room.

"You don't have to fret; I'm not here to hurt you. I'm Sophia, a fairy guardian..."

"Who sent you here? How did you find me?" I demanded.

The fairy paused for a moment, her dark brown eyes watching my every move, before carefully saying, "I...I have been watching over you your whole life. Sixteen years ago, your parents hired me to protect you from the Dark Shadows. I did my best but they outsmarted me..."

"The Dark Shadows? Are they the ones who took me?"

Sophia nodded.

"Why weren't you...If you were protecting me, why didn't you stop them from bringing me here? Where were you when I needed you the most!" I cried in frustration.

Immediately I snapped my mouth shut and drew my attention to the door, listening for any sign that someone might have heard me. Once I was satisfied that no one was coming, I turned back to the fairy, her eyes full of disappointment and regret.

"Throughout your life I've stayed hidden so no one could connect my task to you. But the day you were taken in the village, the Dark Shadows took notice of me and created a distraction so that I was separated from you. By the time the streets had cleared, you were gone. I tried everything to find you. Finally I met up with a spy in the Dark Shadows that I have been working with. The spy gave me your location and helped me sneak in."

My head began to spin as I realized that this fairy, Sophia, was telling the truth. I remembered the day I was taken and now saw a faint image of a small figure hovering behind me.

I had so many questions.

"Who's the mole in the Dark Shadows? Why are they helping me?"

"I cannot disclose that information for fear that they will be killed."

"What about my parents? Where are they? Are they still alive?"

"Years ago, it was said that the Dark Shadows had taken them to one of their extremely secured prisons that is nearly impossible to penetrate. There were some attempts to free them but, they were unsuccessful. Recently, I heard through the great vine that two highly valued prisoners had escaped..."

My heart hammered inside of me with hope and joy. My parents might have gotten away from the Dark Shadows. They might be able to help me.

"Merissa, I must tell you something very important."

With the snap of her finger, a shining gold ring with a single beautifully cut, sparkling yellow gemstone, appeared on my finger. I stared at Sophia in confusion.

"You are a very powerful witch and that is the reason the Dark Shadows have taken you. They plan to steal your magic. If you want to get out of here alive, you have to trust me. Do you understand?"

"Yes, but...What is the purpose of the ring?"

"It is a very old and powerful relic called the Stone of Solomon. Hundreds of years ago there was a man known as Solomon. He too had the same magical abilities as you, using magic without a wand. It is a very rare gift. With no wand, a wizard is defenseless. They have no way to cast spells."

"He created this stone to ease his overactive powers; the same magic that you hold. The Dark Shadows greedily extracted his powers into this stone to contain the magic, but the fairies, the guardians of this land, stole it to prevent the stone from being used for dark magic."

"Although I was warned of the risks, I have convinced the Fairy Council to take the stone out of secrecy and give it to you. The stone will help control your magic until you learn how to use it properly. However, with your magic combined with the stone's imprisoned power, you will be even stronger than before."

I looked at the ring in amazement. This small object could be the key to controlling my casting. It could help me escape the Dark Shadows. I could finally be free.

Out of nowhere I heard the door open behind me. Joy morphed into shock as I quickly turned around to see Evelyn standing in the doorway. It was another check-in.

A look of horror passed across her face as she stared at Sophia in alarm. Evelyn immediately snapped her wand out and began shooting curses at Sophia. The tiny fairy, who was faster, avoided the deadly spells.

Adrenalin rushed through my veins. I began shoving Evelyn towards the door, blocking her momentarily. With strength I had not expected, she thrust me out of the way and pinned me against the wall, only to realize that Sophia had disappeared into thin air. With a cry of outrage Evelyn's attention turned back to me.

"How did it get in here? What have you done!" Evelyn roared in anger.

My adrenalin rush subsided and my throat seemed to close up. I couldn't speak nor could I defend myself. I stood motionless against the wall. The silence that hung in the air seemed to make time freeze.

Evelyn dragged me downstairs where two vampires, a male and a female, were waiting. She pushed me onto the couch before turning to the expressionless vampires with torn clothing and matted hair.

"Vanessa, Brock, keep a close eye on her. We've had an intruder on the premises. I'll put more protective spells around the property before I leave."

The vampires nodded in obedience before Evelyn swiftly walked out the door.

As the vampires turned their full attention to me, I quickly shoved the ring in my pocket hoping it would stay out of the Dark Shadows' reach.

CHAPTER 6

Emma

I landed on the hard cobblestone ground and got off my broomstick. A sudden overpowering feeling of dark magic caused a shiver to run up my spine. I hated being in the part of Sunlight Hollow ruled by the Dark Shadows, but I had no choice. Two vampires came to me with a message from Justin. The Dark Shadows had finally recaptured Merissa's parents; my sister and brother-in-law.

I weaved through the streets before I found Evelyn and Richard surrounding Merissa's parents. As I came closer, I held back a gasp.

Being locked away for sixteen years left them thin and weak. Dirt coated their clothes. Scratches and bruises were all over their bodies, obviously from the escape.

I stopped before my sister, Jennifer, and looked into her eyes. The dedication to a daughter she no longer knew reflected in them. Jennifer would not surrender without a fight.

"I will ask you politely one last time. How did you escape?" said Evelyn as she came face to face with Jennifer.

Jennifer squared her shoulders, looked directly at Evelyn and swiftly spit at her face.

Evelyn swerved backwards with a scream of frustration. The two vampires immediately pinned Jennifer and her husband Herald to the ground. However, Evelyn didn't strike back. Instead, she stood calmly and said, "If they won't speak willingly then we'll have to use another method to get the information we need. Maybe we should bring your daughter here. I'm sure she'll loosen your tongue."

Jennifer looked at me, her eyes wide in horror. I was hoping she wouldn't find out that the Dark Shadows had captured Merissa. She needed to focus of freeing herself at the moment, not her daughter.

I stood rigid, unable to speak. I turned to Evelyn. She stared at me, watching to see what my next move was. After all of these years, she still didn't trust me. To her one mistake was one too many especially when dealing with Merissa. As a high ranking member of the Dark Shadows, she would gain from Merissa's demise.

"Now that I have your attention, you should be able to answer my question. No one has escaped from this prison before. How did you do it?"

Jennifer did not pay attention to Evelyn. She kept her eyes on me, begging me to give any hint that Merissa was safe. I shook my head slightly, unable to give her the answers that she desired.

"Go to hell!" Herald exclaimed; his face full of rage.

Before I even knew what happened, Herald was on the ground moaning in pain as if someone had viciously shoved him onto the stone walkway. The vampire holding him was flown into the air, landing hard on his back several feet away. Evelyn held her wand high, a sick smirk of gratification on her face.

"Some time in solitary confinement might make them talk. Although I would just love to kill the both of you, I think you might be of some use to us. Emma?" Evelyn called.

"Make sure they are sent to another prison where they can be watched. Constantly. I want them alive, just barely, so we can use them against Merissa."

Seeing the fear rising inside of me, Richard answered, "Of course Evelyn. It is the most ideal response to our situation."

Merissa

The need to escape this retched place coursed through my veins. I pulled the handle on the window one last time but it still wouldn't budge. I slammed my fist against the hard glass in frustration and grabbed my wand; ready to fight my way out.

"Evelyn sealed the windows with a spell. They won't open," said a calm, deep voice from behind me.

I swiftly turned to see a tall, muscular male vampire, Brock, standing at the doorway of my bedroom.

I quickly hid my wand behind my back, hoping he hadn't seen it.

"What do you want?"

"I want to help you," said Brock as he peered into the hallway to make sure no one was listening.

My brows drew together in confusion. He wanted to help me? This had to be some kind of trap.

"I'm not trying to trick you," he said, seeing my hesitance.

"I hate the Dark Shadows, probably more than you do. When I was put on this assignment, I knew that this was my opportunity to obstruct their goals. Please, let me help you. We don't have much time."

Brock sighed as I backed away, wary of his proposal. He was with the Dark Shadows. How could I trust him?

"I've been in touch with Sophia. She's waiting for you. I've already subdued Vanessa, but I don't know how long the potion will last."

"Sophia! You know her," I said, my heart pounding in my chest.

Hope flashed inside of me as Brock gave me directions into a certain area of Sunlight Hollow. I would await assistance from Sophia and, with any luck, get out of the Dark Shadow's reach.

"There will be lots of vampires around so you must stay out of sight," said Brock as he guided me down the stairs.

As I left the house I glanced back to see the other vampire, Vanessa, lying unconscious on the ground. The blood inside of a half empty bottle slowly spread across the hardwood floor beside her. A smile spread across my face. Brock had put a sleeping potion in her drink.

Happiness radiated off me as I ran through the open gate and away from the place that held me captive.

A deep voice shouted for me to stop. I glanced down the street to see five or six Dark Shadows, who were guarding the house, racing to catch up with me. However, my pace did not falter. I continued to run in the direction that Brock told me.

As I rounded a corner I slid to a stop. The sight of the small, broken town that stood before me made the hairs on the back of my neck stand up. Vampires seemed to move casually around in the distance as if this were their territory.

I quickly dodged behind an old, crumbling, wooden shack. My heart hammered so hard in my chest that I thought someone might hear it.

He said that there would be vampires, but I didn't think it would be this many. He had to have led me into a trap. Why would he send me into the Dark Shadow's territory?

Shouldn't I be running away from it?

Doubt spread through my mind as I rethought the conversation I had with Brock. A loud voice came from behind the shed.

"I want them alive, just barely, so we can use them against Merissa; make her understand that we will not play any more games."

It was Evelyn's voice. I clenched my hands into fists, trying to stop myself from shaking. He had led me right back to my captors.

A weight pressed down on my shoulder. I immediately prepared to defend myself; my already clenched fists waiting to fly into my opponent's face.

I breathed a sigh of relief at the sight of a tiny fragile figure sitting on my shoulder. Sophia put one of her delicate fingers to her lips, motioning for me to stay quiet.

"It might be better if we get rid of the girl's parents right away. After all, they have caused a tremendous amount of problems. I'd like to have the first bite. Well, of what's left of them. I might be able to get a sufficient amount of blood," said a hoarse voice.

I suddenly peered around the building to see a man and woman kneeling on the ground; their faces a mixture of anger and fear.

I felt like fainting. I had wanted to meet my parents for so long and now it seems that I may never get the chance. Watching them like this made me feel somewhat guilty. I had caused their lives to be turned upside down. I would not let them die because of me.

If I didn't retaliate now, I may never get the chance to make things right.

Without hesitating, I placed the ring back on my finger

for more control and took out my wand. I began to move towards the group of Dark Shadows. Sophia pulled at my hair and yelled for me to run in the opposite direction but I ignored her.

I aimed my wand and thrust a spell at the unsuspecting Dark Shadows. With bad, impulsive aim the spell flew between Richard and Evelyn, smashing into a wall opposite of them.

The Dark Shadows snapped their heads in my direction with a look of horror spread across their faces. At the sight of me, Emma's eyes grew big and her mouth dropped open. Richard seemed to be in a state of disbelief while Evelyn's look of both astonishment and annoyance faded at the sight of the Stone of Solomon glistening in the sun.

The defiance I felt a few seconds ago quickly dissipated and left me feeling weak and defenseless. What was I thinking? I couldn't take on these skilled, dangerous wizards all by myself.

As if sensing my distress, my father took this opportunity to push the vampire away from him and jump for his wand. Before she could defend herself, my father aimed his wand at Evelyn and thrust a spell at her.

Evelyn gasped as the spell smashed her into a crumbling wall. Her body went limp and she fell to the ground unconscious.

Richard shouted for some help as he and his wife threw curses at my parents. However, I had a head start and avoided every curse with ease.

Vampires came running towards the commotion led by a tall, muscular man with dark hair. The man, obviously a Dark Shadow, knelt beside Evelyn as if she were a person of high importance to him, checking to make sure she was all right. Richard shouted for the vampires to go after my parents as he rushed towards me with Emma by his side.

Without thinking, I ran out of the vampire infested town; ran until my legs burned with each step and my lungs felt like they were about to burst into flames. Spells skimmed my body. The loud sound of running footsteps and voices shouting for me to stop never made me hesitate. Sophia's squeaky voice was drowned out by the hammering beat of my heart. I was running for my life.

When the soaring redwood trees from the Palladium Forest rose before me, I finally slowed my speed. Listening for the Dark Shadows presence, I turned around to find no one behind me anymore. I must have lost them. Relief flooded through me as I continued sprinting through the forest with Sophia clinging to my shoulder.

Once I got a safe distance into the forest, I collapsed beside the trunk of a redwood tree gasping for air.

Sophia hopped in front of me looking the angriest I could ever picture a fairy being.

"You've messed up everything! Your parents and I had a plan to get all three of you away from the Dark Shadows reach, but your little heroic act back there ruined it. Now I have no idea if they're even alive and we're in the middle of nowhere!"

Confusion stabbed through me, but I was too exhausted to apologize. My adrenaline rush subsided, leaving me to feel so weak that I could barely move my arms. I just sat against the tree trunk, sucking air into my lungs like it was my first breath in days.

"You should be glad I arranged a second plan to assure your safety in case anything went wrong."

Sophia made a long, high pitched whistle that almost

burst my ear drums. The trees around us swayed ferociously in the sudden strong wind. The small areas of sun that peered through the dense leaves of the trees disappeared. A loud swooshing sound and heavy breathing came from above.

A large dragon landed on the other side of the tree. It's thick, rough golden colored scales shimmered in the sun. Its smooth wings folded perfectly on its back as it sat obediently on the dirt ground.

"She's a golden dragon. Dragons and fairies work side-by-side to protect Elontra. This particular one, Athena, will be protecting you when I can't. You could say that she's my reinforcement."

CHAPTER 7

Derik

I ran as fast as I could to the site of the commotion. Vampires were scattered everywhere; some knowing what they needed to do while others stood around in shock.

A beam of light shot at me in the confusion. I was knocked off of my feet and sent flying down the street, landing hard on my back. A stinging sensation swept through my wrist. I glanced down, watching the slave band fade. I grabbed my wrist, examining it with disbelief. The mark was gone.

Justin's voice called for me. While clutching Evelyn, Justin ordered me to find Merissa. In all of the confusion, Justin didn't notice that I had become unchained from the Dark Shadows' fierce leash. I was free at last.

I hesitated a moment remembering Brock's warning. It was suspicious that Justin only picked me to go after the girl. But through all the commotion his judgment might be clouded. This could be the perfect opportunity for an act of defiance. I'll be out of the broken, Dark-Shadow-ruled town with hopefully no witnesses. This witch could be the only person to destroy the Dark Shadows once and for all. She could be my freedom; the freedom for all vampires.

With a sliver of hope embedded within me, I dashed out of the town. I was so distracted by how I'd find her that I almost didn't see the people in front of me. I dove out of the way just in time to avoid toppling over a pair of Dark Shadows. Emma stood frozen in shock as Richard heaved her out of harm's way.

"Watch where you're going, you useless vampire!"

Richard roared.

"We lost track of Merissa not long ago, but she was last heading towards the forest with a fairy. Now go find her before she gets too far!"

I ran into the forest, using my enhanced sense of smell to pinpoint the girl and the fairy.

As the hours went by, night was creeping up and I slowed my pace. She couldn't be going too much farther tonight. I planned to follow her trail all night and encounter her in the daylight. There was no use scaring the poor girl even more then she must already be.

I trudged through the darkening forest with the belief that uniting both witches and vampires will end the reign of the Dark Shadows forever.

Merissa

Thirst overwhelmed me. I thrust my dirty hands into the cool, refreshing water of the river and drank like I never had before. Who knew a person could get this thirsty? The late-noon heat from Elontra's warm climate rained down on my body as I drank, not helping the dehydration that caused my mouth to dry.

In a desperate attempt to stop the pain, I flung off my shoes and shoved my aching feet into the running river. A momentary sense of relief flooded over them.

"How much further do we have to go?" I complained.

I had been walking non-stop since sunrise and at the moment, exhaustion overweighed my desire to be free of the Dark Shadows.

"Meadow Ville should be at least a two-day walk from here. Probably less if we don't take too many breaks," said

Sophia.

I groaned in frustration.

"Is this city really the best place to lay low for a while? Will it be the safest place for me right now?"

"Meadow Ville is one of the largest and most populated cities in Elontra. It will be harder for the Dark Shadow's to track you there. Your parents also told me to meet them if anything went wrong. If they're heading towards this city then we are too..."

The dragon, Athena, suddenly jerked her head away from the flowing river; sending gallons of cold water splashing around her. A low growl escaped her lips and her eyes scanned the surrounding area in alarm.

Out of nowhere a vampire leaped down from a tree and landed right in front of me. I quickly backed up in fright and took out my wand. I aimed at the vampire ready to shoot him if he came any closer. The Dark Shadows must have sent him to recapture me but I wasn't going back without a fight.

A look of concern passed across the vampire's face. He raised his arms into the air to show that he's not a threat.

"You're the witch the Dark Shadows are searching for. I swear I'm not here to take you back. I hate the Dark Shadows just as much as you probably do. I'm here to help you," said the vampire.

I shot a stream of magic at the vampire; a spell that would temporarily make him unable to lie. I had already heard this same story from Brock. Either the Dark Shadows had made lots of enemies from the vampires or this was a trick. It was too much of a coincidence to have two vampires declare their hatred towards the Dark Shadows within two days.

"How do I know to trust you?"

The vampire paused for a moment. He didn't strain against the spell; he just let what he had to say come out.

"They killed my father and forced me to be one of their vampire slaves. I hate every last one of them and want to see them pay for the misery they caused me. I was told the amount of power you have. You're stronger than every person who had stood up against the Dark Shadows. I know that you're the only one that has a chance at stopping them. I believe that they not only want you for your magic. If they have to, they'll get rid of you, the only person in the entire world, that can stop them. I'll do anything, even give my life, to make sure they are destroyed. I want justice."

I lowered my wand and released him from the spell. I looked toward Sophia for advice. She nodded her head in approval. Athena, who had been on high alert, now looked calm and harmless once again.

"All right. You can come along with us. Are there any other vampires that came along with you?"

"No. The Dark Shadows sent about five trackers out last night, but I diverted them in the opposite direction. Hopefully we won't come across them any time soon."

I sighed in relief.

A loud roar burst through the forest. The booming sound of footprints followed it, making the ground shake so hard that I fell backwards into the dirt. A herd of unicorns came barreling through the tree. Birds flew chaotically into the sky.

Sophia screamed for me to run just as a gigantic Horned Dragon came swooping through the trees. The large, sharp spikes that covered its spine and the two curled horns that pushed out diagonally from its forehead made the dragon seem bigger than it already was. The dragon's massive claws ripped holes into the ground with each step. Its bright, yellow, reptile-like eyes looked as if they glowed off of its pitch-black scales.

Every muscle in my body jerked to life and I dashed out of harm's way. An extremely hot wave of heat from the dragon's fiery breath brushed past my side. But I continued running and never looked back.

Another wave of heat flew inches away from my body. I swerved to the side but went toppling down a long steep hill. Rocks and broken twigs sliced at my skin as I rolled further down. I landed at the bottom of the hill before I knew it, sending pain through my hip.

I could see the Horned Dragon at the top of the hill fighting with Athena. The Horned Dragon was coming closer to death as Athena burned and tore at its flesh. The two dragons were coming incredibly close to me. I slowly got up and was about to move when someone grabbed me from behind. With lightning fast speed I was carried away from the commotion.

The dim forest went by in a blur. Suddenly I was gently placed down on soft grass and surrounded by an area of lush flowers. Ahead of me a waterfall rushed clear blue water into a lagoon. Sunlight poured onto my body. I looked up to see a clear, blue sky with no trees covering it. All around me the tall trees from the forest provided a barrier between the harsh reality that I faced and this beautiful clearing that caused a sense of peace to flow through me.

I turned around to thank the person who saved me. To my surprise, I found the vampire kneeling behind me with a look of concern spread across his face. All the doubt that

I had felt about the vampire was pushed out of my mind. He saved my life.

"Are you alright? Are you injured?" asked the vampire looking over my body for any sign of injury.

"No...I'm fine. Um. Thanks for saving me..."

"Derik. My name's Derik."

I felt myself blush and I shook his hand in a formal greeting. The roar of a dragon echoed through the forest. I jumped to my feet, my eyes wide as they searched the tall trees for any movement. Derik tensed and pushed me behind him for protection. The form of a dragon appeared in the sky and it swooped down towards us. Landing several feet from me, Athena scanned the area for any more threats. A small pressure landed on my shoulder. I immediately knew it was Sophia.

At the moment I felt safer than I ever had before.

. . .

I snapped awake as someone shook me from behind. I turned to see Derik looking frightened.

"What's wrong?" I groaned.

"We don't have much time. The trackers that the Dark Shadows sent after you are nearing us. We have to go."

I lay on the ground in shock until Derik helped me to my feet. The early morning sun provided a sliver of light that shone over the horizon, just enough to see Athena and the tiny figure of Sophia move into the forest on the other side of the clearing.

"Go with Sophia while I distract them," commanded Derik.

"I can't just leave you here to fight those vampires.

They'll kill you!"

"I'm not going to fight them. I'm going to prevent them from going in this direction just like I did the last time."

Derik took a sharp stick from the ground and sliced the center of his palm. Black blood began to seep out of the broken tissue and drip on the grass below him. Derik squeezed his hand into a fist which only made more of the blood flow from the wound.

"What are you doing?" I shouted, looking down at the blood in disgust.

"I need you to use your magic and burn my blood. When vampire blood is burned, it creates the most repulsive smell you will ever come in contact with; almost like a decaying corpse. I've seen what happens to vampires after a few minutes of continuously breathing this in and it is not pretty. You have to trust me with this."

I did trust him. If Derik said this worked before, I believed him.

I took out my wand and aimed at the growing pile of blood strained grass.

"Ablaze," I said.

In an instant the blood was on fire. Derik was right. The smell of burning blood hit my nose as flames spread across the grass. I pulled my shirt over my nose, although it didn't help fight off the disgusting smell that clung to my nostrils.

Derik placed his hand in mine and we walked silently back into the dim woods.

. . .

Evening was upon us and the trackers that the Dark Shadows sent were nowhere in sight. With Derik's highspeed getaway, he had brought me less than a day away from Meadow Ville. I felt the tension slowly drain out of my muscles with each step towards refuge.

Derik abruptly yanked me to a stop and pushed me behind him.

"Who's there? I can hear you circling us. Show yourself!" he shouted into the ever-darkening forest.

A young red-haired girl slowly peeked out from behind a tree. Her eyes rested on Derik and a smile lit up on her face. Derik seemed to relax at the sight of her and his grip on my arm loosened. An expression of recognition passed across his face.

"Do you know her?" I asked.

"Yes. That's Belle. She used to be my best friend before she disappeared from the Underground."

CHAPTER 8

Richard

The two vampires that were supposed to keep watch over Merissa stood before me with a hint of fear on their faces. They had been kept at the house for an interrogation. So far they seemed to know much less information about the events from this afternoon then we did.

Evelyn, of course, was furious with the vampires for letting Merissa escape.

"How could she have gotten her hands on a sleeping potion? How was she able to get that past you?" she yelled.

Though my wife was happy that Merissa got away, I could tell she was anxious. There would be more pressure on us to keep Merissa safe. With our niece within our reach, we could have easily kept a close eye on her, sending her away when it became too dangerous. With Merissa gone, we had no control. There would be little time to react for what the Dark Shadows had planned.

"I don't know! I can't remember much before or after the potion was in my system," squealed Vanessa.

Evelyn groaned in frustration. She turned to Brock.

"I guess your story is the same, isn't it?"

"All I remember is coming here and then waking up on the floor with Justin screaming at me."

"I want these two to be moved to headquarters for the time being. They will be detained inside the perimeters until we have a reason to believe they were innocent in this situation," Evelyn told Justin.

Justin obeyed his wife, nodding his head in approval before leading the two vampires out of the house.

"On the topic of our headquarters, we should at least alert the Masters of the current situation," said Evelyn.

A sudden look of terror washed over Emma's face. Telling the leaders of the Dark Shadows about our repeated mistakes made me squirm in my seat. They were ruthless leaders who stopped at nothing to get what they desired.

"That's a terrible idea! They'll kill us for this! We'll just have to find her on our own and..."

"I saw the Stone of Solomon on her finger. If we tell them how much more power they can obtain, they will have to spare us. We've been observing her for so long that we're the only ones who actually know how Merissa thinks. We would save them so much time in retrieving her."

Even though it was a great risk to take, we could use Evelyn's plan to our advantage. We would be able to have inside knowledge of the Dark Shadow's plans. Their headquarters was where all of the decisions were made. If we could spy on their progress, we might be able to stop them from recapturing Merissa.

. . .

I always got nervous when I came near the Dark Shadow's headquarters. It felt like at any minute the Dark Shadows would see through me and reveal the truth about my alliances.

We passed through the thick, soaring wall that surrounded the perimeter and scurried through the run-down vampire section. I observed another barrier that separated a heavily guarded, high-class sector for the senior level Dark Shadows to reside.

It would surely be difficult to retreat if anything went

wrong inside. The vampires and Dark Shadows would be on us in seconds.

I entered a tall glass building where the Masters are known to spend most of their time. Along with Emma and Evelyn, I took the elevator up to the top floor and came upon a single doorway. I stopped before the door leading to the Master's main office. The thought of how unpredictable the Masters' reactions may be made every muscle in my body tense.

Evelyn took a shaking hand and knocked on the door. A muscular male vampire opened it just enough to see our faces.

"We weren't expecting you three anytime soon," said the vampire in a harsh tone.

"We have some news that the Masters ought to hear," said Evelyn.

The vampire looked us over one last time before opening the door fully and allowing us access to the Masters.

I took my wife's trembling hand as we entered the room. I remembered vividly that this was the same room that we were detained in before the Dark Shadows had forced us to join their ranks and take Merissa away from her loving parents. Its dim lighting and luxurious furniture hadn't changed after all this time. A sick feeling rose inside of me at the thought of that day.

We had been locked up in a filthy dungeon cell for days before the Masters decided to use us to their advantage. Unlike Merissa's parents, they believed us to be more submissive. When we met the Masters for the first time, it felt as if they were playing a cruel joke. They nearly starved us in that cold, dark cellar; trying to snuff out any resistance we had felt. Yet, they looked amused when our weak, trembling bodies were forced into this very room.

They thought they had us wrapped around their finger; that we were too scared to defy them. That was not true. Those weeks in the dungeon had strengthened our intent to save our niece. If there was anything we could do to seek revenge, it would be to continue aiding our family. Merissa represented hope that the world would change for the better. Our sacrifices would not go in vein.

"I'm assuming that something hadn't gone as planned or else you wouldn't be standing here in this room. Am I right?" said a cold voice.

I spun around to see both of the Masters standing before us. Their faces held a somewhat curious yet sadistic expression that made the hairs on my arms stick up.

"Why are you here?" asked Julia.

I cleared my throat and said, "Merissa has escaped again, but–"

Vince growled, "I thought we were clear about what would happen if you failed to retrieve her."

"Wait," shouted Emma fearfully.

"If you kill us and appoint someone else to retrieve Merissa, it will take a lot more effort. We've studied her for months before attempting to capture her. It's just a matter of time before she'll fall into a trap."

"There's also a greater matter upon us. Evelyn claims to have seen her with the Stone of Solomon," I said.

The Masters eyes grew wide with shock. They turned to Evelyn with a look of astonishment across their faces.

"The Stone of Solomon! How…That's impossible!" shrieked Vince.

"It's true. I saw it on her finger in the form of a ring,"

said Evelyn.

"Well I believe you'll be staying around for a little while longer. You may want to get comfortable."

CHAPTER 9

Emma

Each passing day since we came to the Masters I regretted it. There had been plenty of discussions relating to how the Dark Shadows would remove Merissa's magic and what would be done with it. I've even heard some rumors that the Masters were planning to claim Elontra as their own with the aid of Merissa's magic and the Stone of Solomon.

The Dark Shadows suspected a traitor was amongst them. Evelyn had informed the Masters about Sophia and they had grown suspicious. It was starting to get increasingly dangerous for Richard and me to be in the headquarters.

"What if Merissa's fled further than we thought? She could have gone in the opposite direction that our trackers are heading for all we know," exclaimed Evelyn.

I tried to give my best impression of being deep in thought. I knew that Sophia was leading her towards Meadow Ville to meet her parents. However, I now realized that was not the best idea. The Dark Shadows were searching every city, big or small, looking for her. With no possible way to contact the fairy, I had to keep hoping that she knew what she was doing.

"The trackers should be able to tell us. They should be arriving in just a few moments," replied Julia.

As if on cue, the doors to the Masters private office opened. Two vampires that looked like they had been living in the woods for months barged in.

"We've tracked her towards Meadow Ville. It seems like

she had some company. We encountered burnt vampire blood twice and could still smell the lingering aroma of the fairy. There were also some dragon footprints on the ground but it could have been wild."

"You both have been extraordinarily useful today. You may leave," said Vince.

Both vampires immediately dashed out the door. Vince turned his attention to Richard, Evelyn, and me. The wide smile that spread across his face caused my heart to pulsate in my chest.

"This is your only chance to prove to us that it was beneficial to keep you alive. If you bring us Merissa and the ring, then you'll have nothing to fear. But if you fail, you'll regret not running when you had the chance."

CHAPTER 10

Merissa

I stood inside Belle's cabin, peering out of the dust covered window into the dim forest. The branches from the tall trees almost completely covered the cabin, allowing people to pass by without noticing it. Branches and roots hung down from the ceiling, hitting my head every so often as I moved. The cracks in the wooden walls let in a fresh breeze, clearing the air of the moldy smell inside.

We were just on the outskirts of the Dark Shadow's headquarters, though Sophia refused to stay here. Yet somehow Belle had convinced her that I was safe for now. She admitted that she was a rebel in the Dark Shadow's mists. She would do anything, even endanger herself, to hide me if it meant their downfall would arise.

I personally did not think that this was a good idea. I was too close to the Dark Shadows for comfort. It was too unlikely that my arrival in this present safe house would go unnoticed.

But Derik trusted Belle, and I had come to trust him. If he thought Belle would be an asset, then I had to believe he was right. Derik explained how he had grown up with Belle in the Underground. They shared a loyal bond. That had to represent some kind of trustworthiness, didn't it?

"How did you end up here? What happened to you?" asked Derik.

"After the Dark Shadows threatened to seize the Underground and strip our leader, Cyril, of his power, Cyril decided to make a bargain. He took twenty young vampires, including me, out of our beds at night and shipped us off to the Dark Shadows in order to make an alliance."

Derik's hands clenched into fists. The anger in his eyes caused my muscles to tense.

"There have been more uprisings against the Dark Shadows lately and vampires are the ones on the front line. The Dark Shadows are using Cyril to collect vampires for their defenses and in return Cyril gains wealth and sovereignty."

"If this is truly happening, then Cyril isn't the only one the Dark Shadows are benefiting from. There has to be other corrupt leaders that have allied with them; which also means that no one can be trusted," said Sophia.

Suddenly the broken little cabin made me feel exposed. Who was I able to trust now? Anyone could be an enemy.

. . .

I jumped off the couch, startled by the pounding on the front door. My entire body trembled as I inched towards the back to the cabin. Derik and Belle came rushing to my side with a look of horror spread across their faces.

"Belle, open this door!" demanded Richard.

My body froze at the sound of Richard's voice. During the past week I had started to relax; thinking I was safe. Sophia was teaching me how to harness my magic and use it to defend myself. I was beginning to think that my fight with the Dark Shadows was coming to an end; that they had forgotten about me. I was hoping that I could move on; head back into society and start again in another town just like I had done before with my Aunt and Uncle.

However, at the back of my mind I knew it couldn't last.

They would never stop looking for me and now I had been found.

If only we hadn't sent Athena away. She was too big to keep around. She would have been easily noticed. But now that she was gone and I was in danger, I felt like I had made the wrong decision. She would have been fighting the Dark Shadows away immediately.

"Run out the back door! It's your only chance," ordered Belle.

Derik shoved me in front of him and we ran out of the cabin. My heart skipped out of my chest as we clamored through the forest once again.

From behind me, I could hear Richard, Emma and Evelyn burst out of the cabin. Their shouts echoed through the forest as they chased after me. Curses rushed past me but my pace did not falter. Adrenaline controlled my body to the point where I no longer thought about where I was going or how much my legs ached from running. I only wished to be far away from the Dark Shadows.

A spell knocked me off my feet and I went tumbling to the ground. A scream escaped my lips as I slid on the forest floor. I looked around for Derik and Sophia but soon realized that they were nowhere to be seen. We must have separated at some point.

Before I had time to react, the Dark Shadows were upon me. Richard wrapped his arms around me and hauled me to my feet. I lashed out in an attempt to escape but he was too strong.

"Let's get her to the Masters before we have any more interference. I'll send the tracking vampires after that traitor, Belle, and the others," said Evelyn.

Richard dragged me through the forest. I dug my heels

into the damp forest floor, trying to slow him down. But my efforts were in vain. Richard lifted me so that my feet were inches from the ground. I squirmed in his arms as we drew near to a large walled entrance. A vampire opened the large, steel gates, allowing us access into the Dark Shadows' headquarters. I continued to struggle to get away as we passed the hungry vampires. I could feel their eyes staring at me while the Dark Shadows led me into what seemed like a tall, glass office building.

I kicked my legs behind me, feeling my feet make contact with Richard's knee. For a moment, he let me go. I quickly turned to make a run for it, but he had once again got hold of me and put me back into his tight grip. I dug my heels into the marble floor and tried to thrust my body away from Richard. His arms tightened around me and a sharp pain jabbed my side as Evelyn dug her wand into my skin. I stopped fighting and looked around desperately for anyone who might be able to help. I choked back my tears when I only received cold, menacing stares from vampires and Dark Shadows in the lobby.

Richard dragged me into an elevator. I cursed at him and clawed at his hands in a last attempt to break free but it was no use. The elevator climbed up the building and it felt like each floor we passed was another breath stripped from my lungs.

Finally the elevator stopped and the doors opened. Richard dragged me out of the elevator and through a single set of doors to where two people stood in the center of the room.

"Didn't I tell you that we'd find her, Vince?" said Evelyn joyfully.

"You were indeed right Evelyn. I shouldn't have

doubted you for a second," said the man, Vince, as he strode over to me.

He stood so close to me that I could feel his hot, foul breath on my face. Our eyes met for a split second and I could see the desire for supremacy within them.

"Where has she been hiding?"

"She's been hiding with one of our vampires. I believe you may know Belle," replied Evelyn.

"Yes. She led the security patrols along the wall," Vince said with a hint of disgust in his voice.

"Is that the Stone of Solomon on her finger!" asked the woman.

Vince yanked my hand towards him with a look of astonishment and pleasure.

"Julia, come here and verify the stone. I want to make sure it is truly the real one."

The other woman, Julia, strode up to me and lifted my hand so that it was level with her eyes. The tip of her wand touched the stone for a brief moment, making the gem shimmer a bright yellow glow. A devious smile rose upon her face and I yanked my hand back in repulsion.

"You were right Vince. It is the Stone of Solomon! We must get it from her at once."

I curled my hand into a fist as Vince yet again grabbed my hand. He pulled at the ring to try and take it off my finger. I jerked my hand away from his grip and thrust my body backwards, knocking Richard off balance.

Richard let go of me as we both crashed to the floor. I darted away from the group of Dark Shadows and snatched out my wand. In an instant, five wands were pointed directly at me. Sedation spells were thrown into the air in my direction. I tried my best to block them, but I was outnumbered. The spells continuously skimmed my skin making the area feel numb as I blocked and dodged them.

The spells stopped soaring at me and fear washed over the Dark Shadows' faces. Still aiming my wand at the Dark Shadows, I quickly glanced in the direction they were staring. Directly behind me, with the sunset illuminating her golden scales, Athena was flying straight toward the glass walls.

It was now or never. I ran for the door to make my escape. I flung myself to the ground barely inches away from the doorway as Athena came smashing through the window. Pieces of glass sliced at my skin as they flew throughout the air.

Athena stood up courageously tall, taking up most of the room, and blew burning hot fire from her mouth. Focused on the deadly dragon before them, the Masters ignored my presence. However Evelyn never let her sight off of me. With the Masters distracted by Athena, Evelyn lunged for me.

As I quickly tried to get up she tackled me back to the ground. Desperately trying to get her off me, I clawed at her face. Evelyn shrieked in pain as my nails ripped deep gashes into her skin. While distressed by the blood oozing out of her wounds, I knocked Evelyn off of me and bolted for the door again.

In my desperation for freedom I nearly smashed into the elevator doors as I went to push the button. But it was unresponsive. The security must have shut down the power to the building because of Athena's attack. That meant everyone knew the building was under siege and hordes of Dark Shadows and vampires could arrive at any moment.

I glanced around the hall and found a door leading to a staircase. I let out a sigh of relief. I had found my exit and was sure that I would evade the Dark Shadows once again.

Suddenly warm calming air surrounded my body. I collapsed on the floor, feeling my body weaken with every passing second. Fright pierced my mind as I realized that I had been hit with a sedation spell.

My eyes slowly moved back to the room to see that it was up in flames. The Masters had successfully stopped Athena's wrath. A chaining spell was wrapped around her body to hold her in place; the thick metal chains scratching up against her rough scales as she moved. The hard footsteps of people running up the stairs made the hope I had minutes ago vanish.

Everything was blurring. I couldn't fight the spell. The Dark Shadows had captured me once again and this time I had the feeling that I wouldn't be getting away.

Chapter 11

Derik

I felt so stupid for losing Merissa to the Dark Shadows. One moment she was in front of me and the next we were separated by a dense mass of trees. How could I have let this happen? But the past couldn't be changed. I now had to focus on breaking her out of the Dark Shadow's grasp.

We had waited until nightfall to sneak into the Dark Shadow's headquarters. It would be more difficult for them to track us during our escape. I peered around the front of the Masters' building, watching as the crowd thinned out.

The lingering smell of thick smoke clogged my nostrils. Sophia had sent Athena to help Merissa escape. When they didn't return, I knew something had gone wrong. Belle had instructed us that in an attack, all the Dark Shadow's prisoners would be locked in the dungeons while the chaos was being settled. If that was where Merissa would be then that was where I was headed.

I jumped from the top of the wall surrounding the high end sector of the Dark Shadows headquarters, landing on my feet. A sharp pain spread up my legs from the impact. I clenched my teeth, trying not to let the throbbing pain distract me.

I looked around for the security guards stationed around the walls. A speck of light from a lantern shone in the distance, moving in the opposite direction. I waved to Belle, signaling it was safe to come down.

She landed gracefully beside me with Sophia floating above her. She shoved the black hood over her head, concealing her face from any onlookers. By this time all of the Dark Shadows would have known that she was a fugitive. The only way for her to get in was to disguise herself as a Dark Shadow.

"Now is your chance. Make sure you stay hidden," I said.

Sophia nodded before soaring into the air and out of sight. She was to divert any Dark Shadows away from the main entrance with a concealment charm. She had explained it as a mirror like projection that reflects an image. It hides what was really going on behind it; in this case one that wouldn't show us escaping.

We passed the Darks Shadows and vampires who strode around the grounds and anxiously looked up at the sky now and then. Athena's entrance had made quite an impact. The feeling within the headquarters was tense. The Dark Shadows had been thrown off guard, but I doubt they would allow that to happen again. They would be prepared for an attack from the sky from now on.

We walked up to the main entrance of a tall glass building. A guard eyed us as we drew nearer, his gaze suspicious. He put his hand out, signaling for us to stop.

"What is your business here," he asked, tilting his head to get a better look at Belle's face under the hood.

"That information is only for the Masters to know. They are expecting us," Belle said confidently.

"And who's this?" he asked, pointing to me.

"He's my vampire servant. Now move aside. We don't want to keep the Masters waiting," Belle said with her best contemptuous voice.

The guard stood in front of the doors, unsure what to do. Then he moved to the side, pulling the door open for us.

The hairs on the back of my neck stood up as he continued to eye us from behind, skeptically. I scanned the room looking for any sign that the Dark Shadows may act on their suspicion. Yet we walked through the lobby of the building without any interruptions. I looked to Belle who would have picked up on anything unusual. She quickly nodded her head in the direction of a side door, telling me to go that way.

Realizing that I was holding my breath, I slowly released the air from my lungs. I was overreacting. The Dark Shadows had no idea where we had gone and would least suspect our presence to be within their own walls.

We stepped through a metal doorway leading to a dark, winding torch-lit stairwell. My pulse nearly stopped as my overly-sensitive vampire nose took in Merissa's beautiful, sweet scent. She was here! My footsteps echoed down the stone steps as I hurried down the stairwell.

I swiftly jumped back in shock as I landed on the bottom step. Brock stood against the wall looking directly at me. His arms were crossed in what looked like a defensive manner, yet a sincere smile rose upon his face at the sight of me.

"I thought you'd never come, Belle. The Dark Shadows are already in the cell with Merissa. The extraction is going to begin shortly. I made your task easier and cleared the guards out."

Following Brock's gaze I glanced at a corner where two vampires lay motionless on the floor with their limbs fixed in awkward positions. My body stood stiff with shock. Brock was a rebel against the Dark Shadows?

All I could muster out was, "I thought...you..."

"When I told you to be careful around Justin, I meant it.

He had a very good sense about which vampires are radicals or could become them. From the first day I met you I got that vibe. I'm glad you're still alive..."

From the back of the hallway a blood curdling scream pounded through the air. It was Merissa's. The Dark Shadows had started. I sprinted though the dark narrow hallway where the screaming grew louder. I lunged into the cell, unsure of what would lie behind the door.

Merissa

I woke to find both my arms tightly tied down to a chair with thick rope. A small pounding began in my head from the aftermath of the sedation spell and my mouth was dry from smoke inhalation. I glanced around the room I was held in. The pounding became fiercer as dread consumed me. They had placed me alone in the center of an empty chamber that reminded me of a dungeon cell. A single window allowed a sliver of moonlight to pour into the torch-lit room.

This must be where they were going to steal my magic. As soon as someone walks through that barred gateway, it would be all over for me. There's no possible way that I'll survive the extraction. No witch ever has. Losing your magic was like losing a vital organ. One part could not survive without the other.

I began to struggle in the seat, hoping to find a weak spot in the rope. I could feel the ropes tightening around my arms; cutting into my skin the more I squirmed. These were no ordinary ropes, they were charmed to tighten if I tried to break free.

My head snapped towards the sound of the cell door

opening. My breathing quickened as Evelyn walked into the room. She stared directly at me with a hint of rage in her eyes. Only two red, scarred scratch marks remained on her cheek from earlier. She must have mended the shallower cuts I inflicted with a healing remedy.

Richard walked into the room shortly after Evelyn. An expression of regret appeared on Richard's pale face. Was that sympathy I was seeing? That's impossible! He only cared about power just like all of the other Dark Shadows.

"Richard, hold her head steady. Let's see if Cora's potion works after all," said Evelyn as she grabbed a small potion vile from a table behind her.

Richard immediately strode behind me. His rough hands grabbed my jaw, struggling to push my mouth open. I squirmed in my seat as Evelyn came closer. The look of fear in my eyes made her gloating face smile.

Evelyn grabbed my cheeks; her sharp nails digging into my face as she squeezed. I shook my head around, trying to loosen her grip, but she did not let go.

The rim of the glass vile smashed into my teeth, shooting pain through my mouth. I could feel the clear liquid pour against my teeth. I kept my jaws clenched refusing to let the potion run down my throat.

Richard clenched my nose with his other hand, pushing the back of the chair into his body for support. I could no longer breathe. I struggled to free myself from their grasp but the harder I tried the more oxygen I craved.

I was at a standstill. If I kept my jaw clenched, I would pass out and they would continue with the extraction while I was unconscious. If I opened my mouth, they would win anyways. There was no way out of this. The Dark Shadows had won.

I opened my mouth taking in a big gulp of air. The potion rushed down my throat, leaving a burning feeling in its wake.

I tried to spit it out, but Evelyn was quick to cover my mouth. The potion bounced back against her hand and back into my mouth.

"Swallow," Evelyn shouted in frustration as she clenched my nose just as Richard had.

My feet kicked at the floor as I fought against Evelyn's hands, shaking my head in an attempt to throw her off.

Finally I gave in. I swallowed the foul tasting potion. My body lit up like it was on fire; heat radiating off me.

"Let's drain her powers now so we can get this over with. Richard guard the doors while I have the pleasure of stealing her life," said Evelyn with her wand raised.

A bright glowing stream of yellow magic jumped out of my chest and formed a ball around the tip of Evelyn's wand. An unbearable burning pain swept through my body. I screamed at the top of my lungs. I had never felt this much pain in my entire life. My muscles tightened and I clenched the armrests of the chair as hard as I possibly could.

It was as if a part of me was being ripped out of my very soul. I was splitting apart, piece by piece, until a fraction of myself remained.

A curse shot passed Evelyn, missing her only by inches. A look of horror passed across her face as she stared at Emma who was standing in the cellar's opening with her wand aimed at Evelyn. Richard stood behind her with his wand drawn at his side for backup. Evelyn's wand dropped down to her side stopping the extraction spell. The ball of magic blasted back into my body, knocking the chair back into the wall. My shaking body slunk back into the seat. The pain lingered in every inch of me and my face felt wet with tears.

"Drop the wand and back away from her!" shouted Emma.

Confusion swept through me and by the expression on Evelyn's face she felt the same. Evelyn reluctantly let her wand drop to the floor and slowly moved towards the rear cell wall. Her eyes went wide and her mouth dropped open as she stared at my ring on Emma's finger.

"You never gave it to them! You...."

A small spell came barreling out of Richard's wand, hitting the wall close to Evelyn.

"Don't make me do it Evelyn," said Richard.

He kept his wand aimed at Evelyn while Emma hurried over to undo my bindings. Her usually soft touch made my arm flare up in agony. The pain still lingered from the extraction and every movement felt like my skin was about to rip open. A loud whimper escaped my lips as she began untying the knot.

Suddenly someone burst into the cell. The moonlight hit the new intruder and relief flooded through me. It was Derik. My heart pounded with longing for his closeness.

He stared at me like he had been reunited with a long lost friend. Brock and Belle soon joined him, yet his eyes remained on mine. The pain I felt seemed to vanish at the sight of him.

Abruptly, Richard shoved Derik to the ground just as a curse shot in his direction. The cell seemed to roar back to life as Evelyn leapt for her wand and continuously fired deadly curses at anyone opposing the Dark Shadows. The pain once again spread through my body. As I got up from the chair a curse soared towards me. Emma shoved me out of harm's way and rebounded the spell. The curse skimmed across Evelyn's arm as she dodged it, causing blood to soak through the fabric of her dress.

Evelyn screamed out in pain and squeezed her arm to stop the bleeding, dropping her wand again. Belle took the opportunity to lunge at her. She knocked Evelyn to the ground and squeezed her throat. Evelyn reached for her wand, but Brock quickly kicked it away. Evelyn thrashed against Belle trying to push her off. But it was no use. The vampire was much stronger.

I watched as Evelyn gasped for breath until her eyes rolled back into her head and she lay beneath Belle unconscious. Blood still oozed out of the spot where the curse hit. Belle held her breath and quickly turned away as if the smell of the blood might lure her in for a kill.

It scared me that I was willing to watch the light in Evelyn's eyes dim until she could no longer remain awake. Before the Dark Shadows found me, I would never have allowed myself to do such a thing; it would have repelled me. But their cruelty and lust for power had changed me. I was stronger and wiser than I used to be.

Someone tapped my shoulder. Emma held out my wand and ring telling me to take them. I cautiously took my wand from Emma and placed my ring back on my finger.

"I know you don't trust us but in order to get out of here safely you must give us a chance. We have been trying to aid you all along. My husband and I sent Sophia to help you against the Dark Shadows. We know a safe place for you to stay for a while. It's one that only your mother, my sister, and I know about," said Emma.

Richard and Emma were the ones who sent Sophia? They were the moles within the Dark Shadow's ranks.

Emma is my aunt? How was this possible? I thought they were Dark Shadows. I hesitated a moment. This could all be part of the Dark Shadow's plan. No. The Dark Shadows were going to steal my magic and kill me in the process. That was their plan. Emma and Richard had stopped it.

"Sophia will have to verify this once we're away from the Dark Shadows. Now get me out of here."

The smell of the smoke still lingered in the building as we headed up the stairway. Dread for what might have happened to Athena drifted through my mind. I quickly pushed those thoughts down knowing that these worries won't break me out of the Dark Shadow's headquarters.

Derik stayed close beside me, guiding me up the stairs while my body felt sluggish and weak. We reached the building's lobby. I felt a moment of relief. We were going to make it out to safety.

As we made our way across the lobby my full attention was focused on getting out the door. Suddenly, Derik swiftly yanked me back but he wasn't fast enough. I collided with a muscular figure knocking him off their feet. Derik caught me from behind and swiftly pulled me upright.

Terror pulsed through me as Vince bounced back on to his feet and rose before me with his wand raised. A moment of bewilderment passed across his face as he looked from me to my allies. Derik heaved me into his arms and dashed for the door, pushing Vince aside.

"Stop them!" roared Vince.

The night's darkness suddenly surrounded me. For a moment I could only hear the crashing footsteps from vampires as they chased us. I could feel the swift, air-like sensation of spells soaring past me. Slowly my eyes adjusted to the darkness and the sounds from the Dark

Shadows vanished into the distance. I was back in the forest again.

Derik placed me gently on the cool dirt ground. I quickly snapped my head back in the direction we came from. I couldn't see anyone else.

The fear I had felt for the people who had just risked their lives to save me instantly disappeared. Brock and Belle were right behind me, lowering Emma and Richard to the ground. A small figure rapidly flew towards me. Sophia landed on a branch with her chest heaving in exhaustion from a quick flight.

"I need to go back and leave a false trail for the Dark Shadows to follow or by sunrise we might all be captured. We're still too close to their headquarters," said Brock.

"But you won't know where to find us! What if you get captured? They'll kill you!" shrieked Belle.

"One of us would have to do it anyway. Besides, if I die tonight I'll die knowing that my sacrifice was well worth it. If I live, I'll be scouting through the vampire villages for new recruits. I have some friends in Sunlight Hallow that I believe will be honored to join the rebellion against the Dark Shadows."

Belle pressed her lips together tightly, making a quick but serious decision.

"Stay safe and watch out for the Dark Shadows. They might start getting desperate."

CHAPTER 12

Merissa

A dragon's roar echoed though the forest. I snapped my head in the direction of the sound.

"That's the Dark Shadow's dragon encampment. We'll take a detour around it so we can reach Downtown Meadow Ville without running into any Dark Shadows," instructed Richard.

"If Athena is alive, would she be held there?" I asked.

"The Dark Shadows sent her there after she was sedated. But you're not going to risk your life for a dragon. We'll proceed as planned," said Richard.

Fury flashed inside of me. I would not be told what to do especially from someone I didn't trust!

"Athena could have died to save me! She's part of the reason that I'm here with you now and not lying dead in the Dark Shadow's headquarters."

"We wouldn't have let them have you...."

"If you think for one second that I will leave her to die, you are wrong!" I screamed.

Silence spread throughout the group. My gaze remained fixed on Richard's, challenging him to an argument. But, instead of arguing, his gaze dropped to the ground as if embarrassed.

"The dragon is a valuable asset to Merissa. I can guarantee that once Athena is amongst us again Merissa will be protected in a way that none of us can provide her," stated Sophia before turning to me and saying, "And yes, they are on your side. Trust them like you would trust me."

I let out a deep sigh of relief. They were telling the truth.

I wasn't led into another trap.

"She'll stand out far too easily in the city. We'll have to compromise by having her dragon on the borders of the forest where she can guard her from a different perspective," sighed Emma, who obviously didn't believe that freeing Athena was a good idea.

"I don't care about what compromises we will have to make. All I want to do right now is get in, grab Athena and get out of there alive," I said as I marched towards the booming sounds of the dragons.

I followed the roars of restless dragons to a massive stone-walled encampment. My eyes scaled up the thick, moss-filled walls, which seemed to end just above the soaring redwood trees. Richard led the way along the fortification to a wide entrance into the encampment.

The entrance was bare with no one guarding it. My gut told me it was a trap, that I should run while I had the chance, but my stubbornness said otherwise. I owed my life to Athena. She deserved to be free.

"I don't like this. This is too easy. After all that has happened, there should be guards here," said Richard as he peered his head into the encampment, scanning the area.

"I'm not leaving her behind," I said with a hint of annoyance in my voice.

Richard sighed, knowing that any argument would not go in his favor.

"Merissa, stay behind us once we enter the encampment. Richard and I will lead you to your dragon. The rest of you should wait out here in case the Dark Shadow's trackers are led in this direction," said Emma.

"Why should we trust you with Merissa's life? For all we know you're a double spy. I'd rather go in with her!"

argued Derik.

"There is only one way in and out of here. If the Dark Shadows swarm this place and we're all inside, we won't stand a chance."

Derik was going to object, but I argued that it was a perfectly reasonable plan. They could protect us from the outside if anything went wrong. Emma and Richard were the only ones who knew where we were going once inside. We needed them.

Taking out my wand, I entered the dragon encampment. The air seared my skin from the heat of dragon breath. Hard, dry dirt crunched under my feet. Massive cages illuminated by torches populated the encampment's interior. Vampires rushed though the encampment busy with keeping the dragons tamed in their prison.

A glimmer of gold scales caught my attention from one of the cages. I sprinted to the cage until I was face-to-face with Athena. Her head perked up at the sight of me. I had never been so happy to see her. I slid my hand into the cage, gliding my fingers over the smooth scales on her nose.

Out of nowhere Athena released a low growl and bared her teeth. Emma shoved me behind her with her wand raised. My heart nearly faltered as Justin stood before me with a group of vampires flanking his sides.

"As soon as one of our messengers told me you escaped from our headquarters, I thought you might be back for your dragon. It was a lucky guess," said Justin with a devious smile upon his face.

"I've sent a vampire to alert the Masters of your presence. There will be no escape for you this time."

A wall of vampires formed in front of us, blocking any

possible way out. Guilt seized me. I had been so naive. I should have listened to Emma and Richard. The Dark Shadows had expected me to return for Athena. My choice would cost the lives of all of my friends.

"Merissa!" Richard whispered.

I glanced at Richard to see him quickly tap his wand with his finger. What did that mean? Richard tapped his wand again and whispered, "Opening charm."

A light bulb flashed inside of my head. He wants me to release Athena. She'll be able to fight off the Dark Shadows and get us out of here. It wouldn't matter if the Dark Shadows swarm the place. We could fly out with her.

I slowly reached into my back pocket and withdrew my wand, keeping it hidden behind my back. I aimed it towards the cage in what I hoped was the direction of the lock. It would be trial and error. The charm had to enter the lock in order for it to work. I had to be subtle. If the Dark Shadows saw what I was doing, this plan would be over before it began.

"You should have run while you had the chance, girl," Justin gloated, "Once we've disposed of your allies, I'm sure Evelyn would love to finish what she started and we're getting close to doing the same to your Rebel leader."

The charm shot out of the tip of my wand but the cage didn't unlock. I had missed. I redirected my wand preparing to try again. Another charm exited the tip of my wand. The lock still didn't open. The only sound I heard was Athena growl as it hit her instead.

"Your friend Belle hurt my wife and for that I will make sure that she receives no mercy. Evelyn will have her hands full with you so I'll take it upon myself to squeeze the life out of her just as she almost did to..."

I shot the charm again. A sharp clicking ripped through the air causing fear to appear on the vampires' faces. The cage door burst open behind me. Emma shoved me to the side as Athena stepped out from her cage. A look of horror passed across Justin's face as the mighty dragon shot a blast of fire from her mouth.

The area around me soon turned into a scene of glowing, fiery chaos. The vampires who remained unscathed by Athena's blast of fire scattered away; some fleeing while others screaming for back up. Thick clouds of hot, black smoke rose to the sky. Every breath I took felt like it was burning my lungs.

"Emma!" Richard screamed over the loud voices of the Dark Shadows and their vampires, "Lead the others to the safe house. Merissa and I will ride Athena out of this place."

Reluctantly, Emma dashed back towards the only exit. A pang of dread hit me in the gut. I hoped that the exit hadn't been blocked by the Dark Shadows.

With my wand ready, I ran towards Athena. A group of angry vampires slashed at her body trying to weaken her. Out of nowhere I was tackled to the ground. I kicked at my attacker trying to push them off of me. I managed to roll onto my back with my fist ready to punch when their hands quickly wrapped around my neck.

Justin swerved his head slightly to the side, avoiding my fist. His soot-coated fingers pressed deeply into my throat causing me to gag and gasp for breath. My hands instantly went to my neck desperately attempting to free myself from his grip. Black spots appeared in my vision. I knew it would only be a matter of time before I ended up in the same state Evelyn had.

Out of the corner of my eye, I saw Richard aim his wand

at a cage across from me. His opening charm hit its target and another dragon with scales as black as the night emerged from its prison. Justin's head snapped towards the dragon, letting his grip on my neck loosen. I used all of the strength in me to shove him off of me. Richard pulled me back onto my feet. Before I could flee, Justin grabbed my leg pulling me back down.

The dragon Richard had freed blew a wave of fire from its mouth incinerating the vampires in its path. A small flare from the fire blast diverted its path and landed on Justin's leg sending it up in flames. Justin swiftly let go of my leg, letting out a blood-curdling scream and patting at the fire frantically. I didn't look back as Richard pulled me towards Athena.

Athena swung her tail at the last remaining vampire, flinging him into the air. She lowered herself enough for us to climb on top of her back. Athena extended her wings and with a few strong flaps we were up into the air.

Shouts echoed from below followed by curses as we soared past. The Dark Shadows reinforcement had finally arrived. Athena let out a painful roar as one of the curses embedded itself into her leg but her pace never faltered and we continued on into the sunrise.

Chapter 13

Merissa

Athena dove into the ground sending dirt and rubble flying into the air. She gave out a loud painful roar followed by many whimpers. One of her rear legs was stretched to the side with blood oozing out of it.

I jumped off of her, nearly losing my own footing. I stared in horror as black vein like tendrils began to spread through her skin from the wound. Richard was immediately beside me, pulling me away from the dragon.

"What are you doing? Let me help her!"

"Merissa stay back! She's been cursed!"

My breath caught momentarily. My eyes couldn't look away from the quickly growing tendrils racing for her heart. I slumped to the ground in defeat. I had risked everyone's life to watch Athena die anyway.

"Merissa, I'm sorry. There's nothing we can do. This curse cannot be cured and if touched it will spread."

"So what do we do now? Just watch her die?" I cried.

Richard glanced down at me with pity swarming in his eyes.

"It shouldn't be too much longer. After she moves on we must burn her body to stop the curse from spreading."

The next few moments felt like hours. Tears dripped from my eyes as Athena's breathing slowed and she grew silent. Her lifeless body, that was now completely covered in the horrid black tendrils, slumped to the ground.

Richard slowly moved towards the body with his wand raised. A flame shot from the tip of his wand and hit Athena's lifeless body sending her up in flames. I watched the flames quickly consume her until all that was left were bones and ash.

"That curse was meant to infect me as well, wasn't it?" I asked, my eyes never averting from the flames.

"I can't help but think the same thing," muttered Richard.

"We must go before the Dark Shadows find our trail. The smoke will attract them to us."

. . .

The sun dove below the horizon leaving us surrounded by the night. We had walked all day with very little breaks for Richard feared the Dark Shadows would eventually catch up to us. My legs ached from the journey and my eyes threatened to close. Ahead of us, the bright lights of downtown Meadow Ville danced in the night.

"We're very close now. The safe house is in the core of the city," said Richard.

"Won't we be exposed? There are tons of people there. Anyone can recognize me," I asked, my voice hoarse from mourning Athena's loss.

"No. The crowds will make it harder for the Dark Shadows to track you. We can easily get lost in them."

Squinting into the darkness, I followed Richard down a narrow dirt path. I spread my arms out, letting the rough branches and shrubs guide me safely out of the forest.

The dirt covered forest floor soon turned to smooth stone roads. Buildings that seemed to touch the night sky loomed over me. People of all ages and backgrounds crowded the streets making it nearly impossible to move. I wrapped my arm around Richard's trying not to get lost in the crowd.

It felt weird watching all the different races of creatures thriving in one place together. Wizards mingled with werewolves as if they were best friends. Demons strode down the sidewalks like they owned the night; never diverting their glowing red eyes from their path. Everything about the city was different from my small, quaint town of Sunlight Hollow.

Richard quickly directed me through the doors of a tall, old-fashioned apartment building. Inside, the building opened into a grand gold-painted lobby with a wide staircase leading up to a pair of gold-plated elevators. My mouth dropped open at the sight of this magnificent place. Unfortunately, my view was cut short as Richard dragged me into one of the elevators.

The elevator shot up making me fall off balance. Richard pointed his wand at the elevator's controls, mumbling a spell to speed up the machine. The floor numbers rapidly increased until the elevator came to an abrupt stop at the second last floor from the top. The doors flew open and Richard pulled me out and down a narrow hallway.

Richard stopped short at the last door at the end of the hallway. A sliver of light was shining through the bottom of the door. His eyes grew wide with fear. He motioned for me to stay behind him as he approached the door with his wand raised. My heart pounded in my chest. Someone was inside the room. Our safe house was compromised.

Richard put his back against the wall and edged towards the door. He slid his hand over the doorknob and slowly turned it. The knob moved with his hand but shortly came to a halt. It was locked. Richard drew his eyebrows together evidently confused. He motioned for me to move further back. I did so without any further question. This wasn't right. If the Dark Shadows were inside the last thing they would think about was locking a door. What was going on?

Richard pulled out a small, silver key from his pocket and carefully unlocked the door. My breath caught as he turned the handle and swung the door open, bursting into the room with his wand ready to attack. My hands shook as silence spread through the hall. I took out my wand preparing to go in after Richard and defend him from whoever was inside. I stepped forward but faltered when he came out with a smile.

"Come inside quickly," Richard whispered.

I slowly closed the space between myself and the door. I kept my wand at my side ready in case of an attack. I entered the room and stopped in my tracks. Inside the man and women that I had seen prior to my first escape from the Dark Shadows stood before me. They were my parents.

CHAPTER 14

Merissa

"Merissa, my baby, I can't believe it's really you. You've grown into a beautiful young woman," said my mother, choking back some tears.

She took a step forward but quickly moved back as if deciding whether it was a good idea to approach me. I stood frozen in place. An awkward presence passed though the room where no one seemed to know exactly what to do next.

I could see the joy in their eyes from being reunited after all of these years. A burst of hope flared inside of me. I was finally going to get the family that I had wanted for so long.

I felt a longing to run into my mother's arms, to have the feeling of a mother's love and safety wrapped around me. Though, at the same time, it felt like she was a stranger; I had never really known who my parents were.

My mother moved forward reaching out to hold me, but paused, unsure if I would allow it.

We were both feeling the same way; unsure of how to proceed after all of this time apart.

"You must be exhausted. Jennifer, can you show Merissa to her bedroom while Richard and I talk privately?" said my father.

I took my mother's hand and let her guide me the short distance to a bedroom near the end of the apartment. I stared curiously at the two separate beds placed against the back wall as she closed the door behind us. A small window at the far end of the bedroom was open letting the cool night air hit my face and rattle the wooden door of a small closet. My mother quickly strode to the window, closed it and drew the blinds shut to make sure that no one would be able to see inside.

She faced me again and I could see the longing in her face for all the years she missed with me. I slowly approached her, hoping I didn't interpret her expression wrong. When I was within feet of her, she opened her arms. I ran into them letting my mother embrace me for the first time since we were separated so long ago.

"I've missed you so much. There hasn't been a day that goes by that I haven't thought of you."

"I know," I cried letting tears drip down my face.

For a moment, I stood with my arms wrapped tightly around my mother not wanting to let go. But eventually fatigue weighed me down. I wiped the tears from my eyes as she walked to the closet and put a blue nightgown on the bed.

"I believe this will fit you. You look around the same size I did when I use to wear it. I have other clothes in the closet that I hope you could use."

I nodded as I felt the soft cotton fabric between my fingers.

"I'm so sorry that this has happened to you."

I looked up to see tears form in my mother's eyes; tears for all of the years that we had spent apart. My mother had given birth to me only to lose me to the Dark Shadows shortly afterwards.

"I wish that things could be different; that we could have been a family," my mother said as tears streamed out of her eyes.

"I know that I can't change the past, but I want the

future to be different. I want you to tell me all about your life with Aunt Lucy and Uncle Ashtyn; tell me everything I missed. Then I want to teach you some defensive spells; something that will protect you from any more danger. Do you think that will be alright?" said my mother as she reached out and took my hands in hers.

I nodded as tears of joy flooded my eyes.

"I'd like that."

. . .

I woke to the bright morning sun shining through the drapes and onto my tired face. I rubbed my eyes wondering what time it was. I could hear whispering from outside the closed bedroom door.

I shoved the covers off of me and headed for the door. Richard and both of my parents were sitting around a small kitchen table with cups of coffee in their hands.

"I thought they would be here by now. I'm worried that something might have happened to them," exclaimed Richard.

"From what you told me, last night there was a lot of chaos. Emma and the others were on foot and must have had to divert their course," said my father.

"Richard, if they don't show up in a couple of days we'll start looking for them. Don't worry just yet. I'm sure my sister can handle herself," said my mother.

"Wait, the others haven't shown up yet?" I asked, shocked.

My entire body stiffened as the possibility of my friends being dead crashed into me. I should never have gone back for Athena. My recklessness may have caused others their lives as well.

An image of Derik's limp body flooded into my mind making shivers crawl up my spine. I had never felt a longing like this for anyone before. I had grown close to him during our time on the run. It was as if without him in my life I would be missing a part of me.

Tears stung my eyes and I struggled to push them away. I hadn't realized that I had been backing away until my back hit the cool wall. I let the wall guide me to the floor where I silently sat staring at the cold floor.

My mother was immediately by my side, pulling me into her warm embrace. She told me that everything would be alright, that Emma and all my friends would arrive soon. Even though I tried to believe her I couldn't. The odds of all of them escaping last night were too slim.

My father stood up and pulled a chair out, begging me to sit down and eat some breakfast. The smell of bacon and eggs drifted into my nose, but I didn't feel like eating. After turning down the offer for what felt like the hundredth time, I was finally seated at the table staring down at my food.

I shoved a bunch of scrambled eggs into my mouth. My stomach threatened to heave it up, but I continued to eat so no one would worry about me.

The minutes seemed to pass like hours as the guilt for what I had done pulsed through my veins. As the day turned into dusk it became unbearable, not knowing what had happened to them.

. . .

A strange noise came from behind the closed living

room doors. I slowly opened the two wooden, sliding doors to find my father standing in front of a hawk perched on the ledge.

"Hawks are very loyal birds. Your mother and I have been relying on this one to pass messages."

I froze where I was, unable to speak. How had he heard my approach? My father turned to face me. At the sight of my flustered expression, a slight smile grew on his face.

"You know when the Dark Shadows had captured us, we learned a few tricks to help us survive, one of which being to become one with your surroundings. You must see and feel everything around you."

My father turned back to the hawk, letting it take a small scroll of paper into its beak and fly off.

"The other was to make alliances. Inside the prison we were locked away in, we met some wizards. Before they were captured, they were insurgents against the Dark Shadows. They called themselves the Rebels. As it turns out, we both had similar needs. So when their group of radicals broke them out we came along."

"You probably remember the first time we saw each other a few weeks ago in the vampire-infested village. You were never supposed to be there. We had it all planned out. Sophia was supposed to get you out of that house while we distracted the Dark Shadows. Once the job was done and we received a signal, Emma and Richard were going to get us out of there and we'd meet up again at the Rebel's compound..."

"But I ruined that plan just like I ruined your lives," I cried as the reminder of all my losses cut through me like a knife.

"No, Merissa, you didn't ruin it," my father laid a gentle

hand on my shoulder comforting me.

"You just opened a new path to take. Never blame yourself for anything that has happened. This is all a lot bigger than any of us could have imagined."

I looked at him wide-eyed. What was he talking about?

"You're only one piece of the Dark Shadow's plan. Once they gain your powers, they will have an undeniable advantage, but they won't stop there. Right now, they are a growing threat, but soon enough, with the aid of your magic, they will have the strength to do far more damage. They want to dominate Elontra and everyone within it. That is why we joined forces with the Rebels. Before we would have run but now that seems impossible. They need to be stopped. That's the only way to save you."

"Your magic is powerful; one of the most powerful forms of magic this world has ever seen. You are the most powerful witch in the world, Merissa. If the Dark Shadows can take control of this magic, they will be unstoppable; their lust for power will grow to immeasurable heights. You are both a threat and an undeniable advantage to them. They will stop at nothing to get you."

I stared at my father in disbelief, soaking up all the information he just told me. My thoughts were cut short by the sound of a lock opening. I swerved my body towards the sound with my heart racing. My father pushed me behind him, whispering to stay inside the room. He slowly inched towards the front door, his wand out in a defensive position. I heard the door open and familiar voices echoed through the apartment room.

I ran past my father and faltered just before the door. Tears stung my eyes as Emma, Richard, Belle, Sophia and Derik entered the apartment.

Chapter 15

Merissa

"Absolutely not! It's too dangerous. If she gets captured..." Derik stated.

"The Rebels want to meet Merissa and, once we're there, she'll be just as safe as she is here. The journey should take half a day by foot and if we leave at nightfall there's less chance of us being seen," my father argued with Derik.

I rolled my eyes as Derik and my father sat across from each other with their arms crossed. The last few days had been a battle between them and neither was willing to change their minds. It would be up to me to break this feud. I already knew what I wanted to do. I don't want to run anymore. I wanted to fight back. Meeting with the Rebels would be the first step to stopping the Dark Shadows.

I cleared my throat. They both snapped their heads towards me in shock, as if I had magically appeared out of nowhere.

"No one asked me what I want to do," I said with a tiny bit of frustration in my voice.

Derik stared at me with a small, sincere smile upon his face. Since he got back, we had been inseparable and gotten very close. I knew that smile meant that he would support any decision I made, even if it meant giving into this petty argument. My father, however, stayed tense, ready to argue me into the decision he thought was best. In the short time we'd spent together I'd learned that he was a stubborn and cautious man who would do anything to make sure the Dark Shadows never touched me again.

"I agree with my father. I want to meet with the Rebels."

Relief broke across my father's face. Derik looked as if he wanted to argue but bit his lip to stop himself. My mother who sat beside my father on the sofa with a newspaper spread across her lap cleared her throat to get our attention.

"It says here that there had been multiple vampire sightings in this area. The Dark Shadows are getting close. Since you've finally made a decision..." my mother eyed my father like he was a child who had gotten into trouble, "then I suggest that we leave tonight."

"What about Belle and Brock? If they come back here there's a great possibility that the Dark Shadows would capture them," Emma said from behind me.

My mother turned to look at her sister with a puzzled expression. Belle had left in the morning to assist Brock back in Sunlight Hollow. He and a group of vampires planned a rebellion in the vampire-occupied town. Our sources reported that it hadn't gone as well as we hoped.

"Since my job is done and I've reunited you with your daughter, I can let them know where you're heading. I'll also try to keep the vampires away from here. I'll set up some distractions while catching up to Belle," said Sophia.

"Thank you Sophia for all that you've done for us. That would be helpful," said my mother.

Sophia's little wings began to flutter and within seconds she flew out the partially opened window. It was settled then. We would meet the Rebels and rid ourselves of the Dark Shadows once and for all.

. . .

Night approached faster than I thought. My body tensed readying itself for a fight as the cool air brushed against my skin. The silence in the streets gnawed at my ears making me on edge. It was too quiet. This didn't feel right.

The dark gave us cover, but for how long? If the Dark Shadows were in the area, it would only be a moment before I was yet again running for my life and divided from the people I cared for.

My hand moved up the small leather satchel strung across my shoulder, prepared to reach for my wand. I had packed light with only the necessities I needed if we had to run again.

Although my mother had helped me practice conjuring my magic without a wand, I felt better having it with me. It seemed as if a wand compressed the magic into something that was more controlled. I had better aim with it and my magic felt more manageable.

I felt a hand press against my shoulder. I looked back to see Derik gazing down on me with a look of concern. Clearly seeing how tense I was, he asked if I was okay.

"I'm fine," I lied, not wanting to worry him about the bad feeling that was scraping at my gut.

Although I was itching to meet with the Rebels, a part of me didn't want to leave the safe house. It had been the only place in weeks that I had found complete sanctuary since that fateful day when I was captured.

My father's voice broke my thoughts and I was once again thrown into reality.

"Are you ready to go Merissa?"

I nodded my head knowing what was coming. We would once again have to split up. My father, Derik and I were going to go through the city to get to the Rebel's headquarters. My mother would then lead Emma and Richard into the outskirts of Meadow Ville and meet us there.

I hadn't liked the idea of splitting up but, it was necessary if we wanted to avoid detection from the Dark Shadows. We were too big of a group to be seen together. It would attract too much attention, especially at this time of night.

As the three of us moved toward the dancing lights of the city center, I looked back at my mother, Emma and Richard knowing very well that it could be the last time I ever saw them. For a moment their bodies were illuminated by a streetlight, making them look ghostly white, and then they dissolved into the darkness.

I turned my head back toward the direction I was heading, keeping my eyes open for any trouble that could be lurking ahead. We moved in the shadows of the buildings until we came upon the entertainment district where lights from the buildings seemed to illuminate the entire street. Crowds of people mingled with each other as they entered the clubs and bars lining the street. Bodies bumped into me from all different directions as I tried to squeeze my way through the crowd. Music blasted in my ears from open doorways which made the voices from the crowd almost inaudible.

Derik shouted into my ear, "Take mine and your father's hand so we don't get separated."

I nodded and did as I was instructed. With my father in the lead, we maneuvered our way through the mass of people ahead of us.

Finally, I could see the crowd thinning in the distance.

The clubs and bars were replaced by shops and business towers, though it was still busier than I would have expected. I had almost made it through the thick crowd when a hand grabbed my shoulder. I was thrown back into the packed street making me lose my grip on my father and Derik.

I screamed and tried to keep Derik's hand in my grasp, but the crowd seemed to have already filled the gap between us. The noise from the street was replaced by the violent beating of my heart. Another hand clutched the back of my shirt as I was forced through the crowd. I thrashed my arms back at who ever had grabbed me trying to push them away. My plan backfired and they grabbed my arms instead securing their grip on me.

I was forced away from the clubs and music and into a dark alley between two buildings. The people that were lingering in the alley took one look at my attackers and fear broke across their faces. They ran down the alley like their lives depended on it and onto another busy street. Nausea overcame me as I heard them shout warnings to anyone they could that the Dark Shadows were coming. Within minutes, I could see groups of people scattering in different directions away from us. No one was going to come to my rescue.

I put all my weight onto my right side and threw myself at one of the Dark Shadows. Their grip loosened and they let out a curse as they smashed into the side of the stone building.

I made a run for it, but the other assailant quickly pulled me back and held me against the wall facing them. Shivers rushed up my spine as I stared into Vince's cruel brown eyes. The cold tip of his wand pressed against my neck. I gripped the stone wall behind me tightly, preventing myself from lashing out at him. It would only get me injured, or worse, killed. Unlike the rest of the Dark Shadows, the Masters had the power to decide if I have become a threat that needs to be eliminated. I had to play by their rules until I find the right moment to run.

"Are you alright Julia?" called Vince.

Julia, who slowly came towards us rubbing her sore arm, replied, "I'm fine. Let's get moving before her friends find us."

There was no hiding the frustration in her voice. She aimed her wand at me making sure any escape back to the crowd would be useless. Vince yanked me away from the wall and pulled me down the alley once again. He forced me to turn a corner onto an empty street. I sharply inhaled at the sight of three vampires waiting for our arrival.

"Kevin, bind her so our journey back to headquarters goes smoothly," ordered Vince as he shoved me into the vampire's grip.

The vampire, Kevin, took a long piece of rope from one of the other vampires. He tied my wrists together while leaving an extra bit to be used to pull me like I was a dog tethered to a leash. For a second our eyes met, mine pleading for help while his glowing with delight about my capture.

"See how easy this was. We should have done this years ago! If you want something done right you have to do it yourself," exclaimed Julia.

"Agreed...You there!" Vince pointed to another one of the vampires, "Go up ahead to make sure the street is clear. I don't want to run into any problems."

Without hesitation the vampire left with incredible

speed down the cobblestone street. Vince then focused on my outstretched hand with my ring placed on it. I knew what made his face beam with satisfaction. He wanted to finish what he started in the Dark Shadows headquarters and take the ring; his sick desire for control about to be achieved.

As he approached, I tried to yank my hands away but Kevin held on to the rope with such strength that it wouldn't budge. Vince slowly gripped the ring and began pulling it towards the end of my finger, all the while staring at me with a smug smile. I clenched my hand into a fist preventing the ring from going any further.

"You are in no position to fight Merissa. Let the ring go and give me what's rightfully mine..."

A loud explosion erupted from ahead where the vampire had gone just recently. The flames which seemed to come from a few blocks away lit up the night. From the other side of the alley, screams from the now panicked crowd echoed in the air. Vince jolted away from me staring in shock at the boisterous flames.

Out of the corner of my eye, I could see a figure approach from the alley behind me. I stood there frozen as someone smashed Kevin onto the ground rendering his body limp and unmoving. Kevin's hold on the ropes released, letting me free from his grasp. A spell that came from above hit the last remaining vampire in the chest making him fall to the ground unconscious.

Vince and Julia swiftly reacted and deflected the spells being thrown their way.

"Where did they come from?" Julia exclaimed anxiously.

They quickly backed towards the alley where we came

from. As soon as they were within reach they darted down the alley, fleeing the scene before it was too late.

A hand grabbed the rope and spun me around to face them. Brock quickly ripped off the ropes binding my hands, looking at me anxiously.

"Are you hurt? Where's Derik?" he asked.

I stood there frozen in time as everything played in my mind, but the sight of someone moving on one of the roof tops made me snap back into reality.

I let out a scream and backed away from Brock only to fall on my back. Scooting on the ground, I continued to inch back trying to get as far away from the danger as possible.

"Merissa, it's okay. He's with us," said Brock, taking my hand and pulling me back onto my feet.

"John's one of the Rebels' soldiers."

I paused, looking at the man perched on the roof of the small building. John gave a friendly wave before disappearing to what I assumed was a way down to us.

Relief flashed inside of me as I saw Belle run up the alleyway from the direction of the explosion.

"Is she alright?" Belle asked.

I flung myself into Belle's arms, thanking her for saving me yet again. I was glad that Belle and Brock were alright. After hearing that their rebellious plan had gone astray, I was worried for their safety.

Before I could say anything Belle's body tensed as she stared at something behind me. Belle threw me behind her as she and Brock prepared for a fight.

I could hear it now. Footsteps echoing down the alley that Vince and Julia had fled.

I went to grab my wand but stopped as I heard my father and Derik calling my name. I grabbed Brock and

Belle's arms making them face me.

"Stop! It's okay. It's my father and Derik," I said as I slowly walked toward my father's voice.

For a moment both vampires looked at me, both startled and in disbelief. Then they let out a sigh of relief when my father came running up to me checking for injuries and saying how he should have been more careful.

"It's alright. It wasn't your fault. You couldn't have predicted that they were waiting for us. If it wasn't for Brock and Belle I would have still been caught in their trap," I told him.

My father walked around me towards Brock and Belle. He shook both of their hands while thanking them profusely. I walked over to Derik who stood over Kevin's body looking confused and angry. As I got closer I could see the vampire's chest moving up and down still breathing.

"Do you know him?"

"We were introduced to each other when I was first enslaved by the Dark Shadows. Something seemed off with him though. Unlike the rest of us, he seemed proud of what he was doing. Did he do that to you?" Derik asked with bitterness in his voice as he stared at the marks left on my wrists from the rope.

I didn't say anything, knowing it would only intensify his anger towards this vampire. He made a move towards the unconscious vampire. I pulled him back knowing that killing him in this state would make him no better than Kevin.

"He's not worth it. Let's go before anything else happens," I said.

Derik looked at both me and Kevin, debating his next move. Just when I thought I would have had to pull him back again, he let out a huge breath and his muscles relaxed.

"You're right. Let's go and get to the Rebels camp before they come back."

CHAPTER 16

Merissa

As the morning sun broke through the dark, cloudy sky in the damp forest, Brock signaled for us to stop. Through my tired eyes, I peered around to see what had caught his eye. We had stopped in front of a high, steep rocky slope.

John told us to wait where we were as he slowly stepped towards the entrance. He knelt in front of a large bush pressed against the slope. He pushed some of the branches out of the way and whispered something that was inaudible to the rest of us. I took in a quick breath as I saw a sliver of a man's face through a crack in the slope. His face was painted in the same camouflage colors as John wore and his wand was aimed straight at us.

After John finished speaking, the wizard disappeared into the mountainside. For a moment, I wasn't sure what was going on but then a boulder began to roll sideways revealing an entrance into the slope. Three men in the same camouflage uniforms as John came out from behind the boulder, panting after having used their strength to clear the entrance.

John told us to quickly move through the entrance but I stood where I was in bewilderment. My legs refused to move. The Rebels' ability to conceal their headquarters and security measures shocked me. It had been a long time since I felt as a safe as I did at that moment.

Derik took my hand and guided me to the entrance, noticing that I wasn't going to move on my own. Being the last person to enter, John walked behind us looking back into the forest to make sure that we were not being followed. As soon as we were inside, the three men strained again to move the boulder back to its original position and conceal the entrance to what I could now see was a tunnel.

Once the boulder completely covered the entrance, we were surrounded by complete darkness; the sun blocked from entering the tunnel. Out of nowhere the tip of a torch beside me exploded into bright flames. Then one after the other, more torches lit up along the walls making a visible route leading further inside the tunnel.

I kept Derik's hand in mine as we followed John down the torch lit passageway. I was speechless. I had never seen anything like this. Everyone in front of us suddenly stopped. I peered around to see a tall iron gate with more guards stationed on the other side talking to John. As the gate opened, John turned back to us.

"Our second line of defense wants to quickly search your bags before you enter, as a security protocol. Once they're done, I'll show you to your bunks and you'll then be free to wonder around," John stated.

I followed Derik through the gate and one by one we each willingly gave our bags to the guards to be searched.

"I'm sure you must have already guessed that the design of this compound was taken from the Underground," said John as he closed his hand upon Derik's shoulder, making him turn around.

"It does remind me of home," Derik replied with a smile.

John laughed as he moved along. He told us that he was taking us to the bunks where we will be sleeping. The guards gave us our bags back and we followed John.

The tunnel began to widen around us until we entered a massive underground chamber made of hard, wet rock.

Around the border of the chamber were more tunnels leading in different directions. Rebels of all different backgrounds filled the chamber, talking amongst themselves and sitting on flat portions of outstretched rock that was carved into benches.

As John led us through the crowd along the edge of the chamber, I peered down some of the tunnels. Some led into smaller chambers filled with metal bunk beds, while others were used for dining and meeting areas. Not all the tunnels were used though. Some seemed to have no end, possibly used as an escape route.

I followed John into one of the small chambers filled with bunk beds.

An old book on the bed in front of me caught my eye. My eyes grew wide when I recognized the creased and faded cover. This was my Aunt Lucy's favorite book. 'The Tales of Otherworldly Non-magical Beings' would have been insignificant except for the very poor condition it was in. It was in the same condition Aunt Lucy's was in.

The red stain from when I had accidently skimmed the book with paint when I was four made my heart skip a few beats. The waterlogged pages from when it had dropped off the outdoor table into a puddle while she was chasing me around the backyard solidified the fact that this was her book. She must be here.

Before I could say anything, John spoke: "This is one of the newer housing areas that we have cleared out for refugees. You can pick any bed that isn't occupied. I know finding your way around here can be confusing so we have signs on top of every housing chamber's entrance. This is room H11. You're free to look around the compound if you wish."

As John left us to settle in, I heard a gasp behind me. I turned quickly towards the sound. My breath caught making it feel like I couldn't breathe. Pure joy spread through me as one of the people I thought I had lost since I was taken by the Dark Shadows stared at me with the same look of confusion and happiness.

I leapt into my aunt's arms. Tears sprang to my eyes. I had thought I would never see her again. My cheek felt wet against my aunt's, not only from my tears, but hers as well.

Aunt Lucy let go and clutched my face, staring at me with her warm, teary eyes.

"I thought I had lost you forever. These past few months had been a living hell for both your uncle and I. But it must have been worse for you, being taken by the Dark Shadows. I'm so sorry this happened..."

"It wasn't your fault. It was mine. I should have listened to you instead of taking your word for granted," I sobbed.

"I won't let anything happen to you again. They'd have to go through me to get to you," Aunt Lucy said with a hint of anger in her voice.

From the serious look on her face I knew she meant it. She would sacrifice herself to save me, just as a mother would do to protect her child. As a matter of fact, she was a mother to me, not by blood, but from raising me when mine had been imprisoned. My aunt and uncle had been the only family I had.

With that thought, my uncle, a tall, slender man with short, blond hair, entered the room anxiously looking around. As his eyes locked on my father, he shouted his name. Uncle Ashtyn ran up to my father sweeping him into a tight hug.

"It's been too long, brother. I have prayed for so long

that this day would come," said my uncle.

"So did I, Ashtyn," replied my father.

Uncle Ashtyn turned to me with his arms open. Without thinking, I ran into his arms like I had done when I was a kid. He squeezed me so tight that for a moment I felt like I couldn't breathe.

As he let go, Uncle Ashtyn cupped my face in his hands staring into my tear-filled eyes and said the three words that I desperately needed to hear since I was taken.

"You're safe now."

· · ·

Although I had my parents back in my life, I still was very attached to my aunt and uncle. I had spent the vast majority of my life with them and, in an instant, we were separated. I thought I would never see them again. But a part of me felt that I was neglecting my parents. It wasn't their fault that they weren't around. They had been imprisoned because of me.

I spent time with my parents to show them that I did care about them. From the moment my uncle disclosed to me at a young age that they were not the ones that gave me life, I fantasized about what my life would be like with them. But I was always drawn back to Aunt Lucy and Uncle Ashtyn.

My parents explained to me that they knew what I was going though and didn't blame me. My Aunt and Uncle had raised me and it was only natural for me to feel this way. That still didn't make the guilt go away. I did love my parents but, the love for my aunt and uncle was stronger. There was no denying that.

A few weeks had passed since I arrived. Since the sun could not penetrate the mountain side and the Rebels thought it best for me to not go above ground, it had been hard to tell time. I had been longing to see the sun again. However, my desire to stay hidden from the Dark Shadows kept me from attempting to break the rules. I would not make the same mistake again.

I was told that the Rebels' leader, Darius, wanted to speak with me. My experience in the Dark Shadow's headquarters and all that I've encountered could help them plan an attack. So far, I hadn't heard anything from him. Apparently, he had been busy with a raid that backfired. I was beginning to believe that he had forgotten. It had been about a week since the Rebels advised me about this meeting.

I sat on a smooth rock budging out of the tunnel wall. Derik was describing to me how this was luxury compared to the Underground. The steady flow of food, water and clothing was something he rarely had. The vampires had lived in the Underground to hide from the Dark Shadows and I seem to be doing the same. The only difference was that I was living with people willing to fight instead of running from my fears.

"My father was murdered by the Dark Shadows and that's why I came up to the surface. I wanted to avenge him. That's when I got enslaved and..."

"And you met me and continued to fight them; just not the way you had planned," I said knowing where the rest of the story was headed.

His smile made my heart skip a beat. He wrapped his arm around me as I sunk into his warm embrace. Every time I saw him, I couldn't help but smile. I had wanted to tell him how I felt for a while now but, I've been too scared of rejection. He was one of the few people that had helped me at the beginning of my escape. I trusted him with my life and cared for him in more ways than I thought I could.

"Derik," I said looking up at him.

Fear made me feel as if I were going to faint. I tried to choke up the words but couldn't. Then I thought about what I had been through. This was nothing compared to the events I had encountered. Even if he doesn't feel the same way about me it will not be my undoing.

Derik looked at me with his brows furrowing. I took a deep breath and said the words out loud.

"Over the time that we've been together, I think my feelings for you have grown. Not just as an ally or friend. I think...I'm falling in love with you. "

He stared at me for a second; his eyes wide. Then a large smile spread on his face. He laid a kiss on my forehead.

"I feel the same way. Not being with you or knowing that you're safe kills me. I love you too," he said letting me lean into him again.

As I rested my head on his shoulder, I saw someone coming down the tunnel. Out of the corner of my eye I watched John stride towards us.

"Merissa, Darius is ready to speak with you."

CHAPTER 17

Derik

Darius, a grey-haired, muscular man dressed in camouflage, just as the rest of the Rebels, was waiting for us along with Merissa's parents, Lucy and Ashtyn. He rose from the long metal table to greet us, holding out his firm hand for me to shake.

"Derik! Merissa! I'm sorry to have kept you waiting for this long. We have been compromised in the majority of our camps. The Dark Shadows have taken an advantage and we believe there might be a mole in our mist. I'm sure you understand the importance of the situation. Now come have a seat," Darius said cheerfully while motioning to the two empty metal chairs closest to us.

The room echoed the sound of war. The dark, torch-lit cave walls and the metal table and chairs made the room seem serious, like this meeting would determine if we lived or died.

"Merissa, I know you've been through a lot and want to get away from all the chaos, but that will only happen when the Dark Shadows are defeated. They will never stop coming after you."

Darius paused, seeing the troubled look on Merissa's face. We all knew it was true. The Dark Shadows have never been so captivated with anyone before. I slowly reached my hand out to hold hers. I could see in her eyes that there were a lot of thoughts racing through her mind.

I too, felt the pressure of this situation. There were so many opportunities at our disposal and it was a challenge to find the right one. We could run, which would only continue the Dark Shadow's chase. Or, we could stay here for a while longer until our debt was to be repaid and we fight alongside the Rebels. Both were risky but only one gave me hope of a peaceful future.

"As you know, this sanctuary does not come without a price. We will need you to aid us in defeating the Dark Shadows. I strongly feel that with your extraordinary powers on our side we will finish this long battle. We need you Merissa. You are the most powerful of all of us..."

"And what is the difference between you and the Dark Shadows then?" Merissa interrupted.

Darius' mouth fell open in shock. Merissa leaned back in her chair, her arms crossed and with a look of dissatisfaction.

"What do you mean...we are very differen..."

"I thought you would be too, but I'm seeing the same plans just with different people. Both you and the Dark Shadows want to use my powers for your own goals. What will happen to me after the Dark Shadows are defeated? Will you continue to use me to gain more power until you become the very thing you fought against?"

Darius looked puzzled for a moment, considering what Merissa had just said. Then he gave a sign of understanding.

"I see where you are going with this. I give you my word that once we bring the Dark Shadows down you will be bothered no more. You will be free to live your life as you wish. I am not and will not use you for what you can do. That is the difference between us. I am giving you a choice in the matter. You may turn down my requests, if I have any at all, and as long as the Dark Shadows are at large, you will be protected from them."

A smile, something that was rarely seen, lit up on Merissa's face. She turned to me, wanting to see what I thought. I nodded my head in approval.

"I'll take you up on your offer, Darius. I'm ready to start whenever you are."

Finally, my goal was going to be achieved. I did not come up to the surface for nothing. We would take down the Dark Shadows. My father and everyone else that was hurt in their wake would be avenged. No one would have to live in fear any longer. We would all be free; free of the cloak of darkness that the Dark Shadows had laid over the land.

However, for some strange reason this act of retribution felt different than what I had expected it to be. When I left home, I was out for revenge. I was angry. Then when I met Merissa everything changed. I found purpose again. I was not fighting on behalf of the dead. I was fighting for the people I cared for.

I could see past all the anger and hate and found a bright new world, a world full of joy and happiness. A place where I could settle down, have a family, live the rest of my days without fear and pain. I had hope for a better life.

We spent the next few hours poring over every detail of the night I rescued Merissa; how to get into the complex, where the guards were stationed, where the Masters reside. Merissa gave specific details about how she witnessed the Dark Shadows operating and any information she might have heard while in their presence.

"Thank you for your time. You've given us a tremendous advantage. We will be in touch with you when we plan our attack," Darius concluded.

"First, we must go over the information with our

informant. Hopefully he's found his way alright. He's been dealing with John for the last month and we finally feel confident to bring him here."

Darius opened the metal doors to let us out. As I walked out of the room a vampire I had known from the Underground rose from a bench across from us, his dark hair and black eyes unforgettable. He was the person who had sent my father above ground only to get him killed. He was the vampire who sold out Belle to please the Dark Shadows.

Shock rushed through me with such force that I felt as if I couldn't breathe. Cyril, the vampire who made a deal with the Dark Shadows, an informant? The Rebels had been fooled. He was not their mole. He was the Dark Shadows' spy; a double-crosser. He would never betray the Dark Shadows. He was one of the most powerful vampires in their reign.

Suddenly, it all made sense. Darius had said that they had a mole in their midst and he was in plain sight this whole time.

Our eyes met, both wide in alarm. Within an instant he was hastily scurrying away.

"Cyril! Where are you goi...."

"He's not your informant. He's only ever allied himself with the Dark Shadows. He's the mole."

"That's a large accusation..."

"Belle will confirm it. She's told you that one of the vampires in the Underground was trafficking vampires to the Dark Shadows. It's him!"

Darius' lips moved but, no words came out. It was as if he were frozen in place, unable to comprehend this information.

"Seal the doors," shouted John, "Don't let him get away."

A swarm of wizards in the area whipped out their wands and surrounded the lone vampire, giving him nowhere to run. I could see in their faces the fear and anger at the turn of events. Cyril stopped, his hands raised in surrender.

"How could you. I...I thought you were fighting for your people...to bring them out of hiding...," Darius stuttered.

"Why would I fight a losing battle? The Dark Shadows will rule this world and I have merely found an opportunity to gain more than I could possibly imagine. Give up Darius. You've lost. Trackers have been following me here and soon the Dark Shadows will be on their way. Thanks to me, I will have given them everything they desire at once; the destruction of the Rebels and the most powerful witch in the world."

Two wizards rushed behind Cyril and grabbed his arms, dragging his away.

"You're a monster," Merissa shouted in anger.

Cyril's laughs echoed throughout the chamber with a menacing tone.

"Lock him up securely in the cells. I want everyone to pack their belongings and evacuate immediately," yelled Darius across the now large crowd.

I pulled Merissa towards the bunker. We were compromised. The Dark Shadows were on their way to reclaim her.

From behind me Cyril's booming voice echoed through the compound, "You're too late. The Rebels will be no more!"

CHAPTER 18

Merissa

I shoved my clothes back into my satchel. My heart was beating out of my chest. The Dark Shadows were on their way. Would I ever be safe?

It felt as if I were a exposed deer, cornered by a hungry pack of wolves with no way out in sight. But unlike that deer, there was a possible way out. There were undocumented tunnels leading away from the cave.

The plan was to evacuate through those tunnels with several groups moving in separate directions. We would meet back up at an old, abandoned, underground shelter where some vampires used to hide until a few centuries ago. This way we all wouldn't be vulnerable when the Dark Shadows arrived. They couldn't catch all of us if we split up.

Derik came into the room, anxiously walking towards me.

"I'll be heading out with your parents. Are you going to be alright? Are you sure you don't want me with you?"

I did want him with me. I didn't want to be separated from Derik ever again, my heart longing for his closeness. But, that feeling was conquered by the one to keep him safe. He was already on the Dark Shadow's radar after freeing me. We would be two targets travelling together.

"My aunt and uncle had kept me safe for sixteen years. I don't think that they are going to give up now."

Derik frowned, trying to get rid on the undeniable urge to stand by my side.

"Ashtyn and Lucy are waiting for you in front of the

first tunnel. Don't take too much longer."

"Done. Let's go!" I said as I shoved my last shirt into my bag and walked out of the room.

I held onto Derik's hand tightly as we moved through the panicked crowd. People were running through the chamber, either rushing to warn their families or heading for the safety of the tunnels.

I could see my aunt and uncle up ahead, standing on a large rock searching the crowd. My eyes met with my uncle's. He pulled my Aunt Lucy down from the rock as he briskly walked toward us.

"We need to go now. We'll need as much of a head start as we can get," said my uncle.

I looked at Derik, full of concern.

"Don't worry. I'll see you at the meeting point," he said as he laid a quick kiss on my forehead.

I watched as he disappeared into the horde moving towards the escape tunnels.

Our tunnel was straight ahead of us. I held on tightly to my aunt's hand as we became one with the crowd. Heat swept across my skin from the massive amount of scared, panicked people around me. My eyes adjusted to the dark as we moved into the gloomy tunnel, with only slivers of light from the random torch that someone was holding.

Out of nowhere, a loud booming sound came from above us. The roof of the tunnel shook violently, sending dust and small chunks of rock raining down on us. Screams echoed through the tunnel as horror rushed through people.

I could hear the shouts of the guards bouncing off the walls of the tunnel.

"They're here! Prepare yourselves to hold them off as

long as possible!"

For a moment, it felt as if I couldn't breathe. Cyril's warning had come true and faster than I thought possible.

"Merissa, push through the crowd now. Try to get out as fast as you can," called Uncle Ashtyn.

Hearing my uncle's warning, Aunt Lucy gripped my hand even tighter than she already had, strong enough to cut off my blood circulation. She shoved people out of the way as we pushed on through the terrified crowd, hoping against all odds that we would make it out before the Dark Shadows find their way in.

Chapter 19

Merissa

Like the entrance to a cave, the dim gloomy light entered the dark passage from the tunnel exit opening up from the ground. Small drops of rain dripped on my head from the dark sky above. The sound of the pelting drops of water hitting the leaves of the trees echoed all around me. Relief swept through me. I was out and, shortly, would be away from the Dark Shadow's grasp once again.

Aunt Lucy and I caught up with Uncle Ashtyn, who was pushing the horde of people aside to find us. Uncle Ashtyn grabbed my hand and pulled me through the forest, following in the wake of the scared mob of people running for safety.

"We need to move faster. Please keep up Merissa," said my uncle as he swept me through the forest.

My short legs couldn't keep up with his long ones. I kept stumbling across the forest floor, my aunt behind me to pull me back to my feet.

"You need to slow down! She can't keep up," said my aunt.

"We can't. They're already here and if we stall...."

My uncle stopped dead in his tracks, bringing me skidding to a halt behind him. Out from behind the bushes hooded figures emerged, their wands raised.

"We've found her, she's here," one shouted.

The sight of the hooded figures knocked the wind out of my chest. More figures emerged from the forest, surrounding us. People were running in all different directions, panicked. Streams of light from cast spells lit up the forest. Some people chose to fight, dueling the Dark Shadows the best they could. Others ran for their lives while some unlucky ones lay motionless on the forest floor.

It wasn't long before more Dark Shadows came to join the fight.

A spell shot at me from one of the Dark Shadows who was running through the crowd, its bright red orb lighting up everything around it. I quickly drew my wand and swung it, deflecting the blow.

"Merissa, run!" shouted Uncle Ashtyn, as he drew his wand as well, averting the spells that were thrown his way.

Although my head told me to run, my heart said otherwise. I took a few steps forward, blocking the spells as they came. I would not leave my aunt and uncle. They were my family, the ones who raised me. I loved them with all my heart and would never leave them again.

Again and again, the Dark Shadows came, sending what I could only assume to be sedation spells at me, they merely meant to capture me, not harm me. Out of the corner of my eye, I could see Justin, his wand raised and a spell being cast by his silently moving lips. There wouldn't have been enough time to react. It all came too fast.

I closed my eyes, preparing for the strong, hard feeling of the spell to knock me to the ground, just like it had done so before. Then, all of a sudden, someone pushed me to the ground, landing on top of me. Aunt Lucy panted, struggling to fight off the spell.

"Run! Get out of here!" she yelled with all the strength she had left.

I could see the fear in her eyes. She was pleading for me to leave them behind, pleading for me to get to safety.

I rolled my aunt's weak body to the side and looked up

to see Justin running in our direction. I shot a few spells his way, giving myself a head start as he pursued me. He threw more sedation spells at me. I turned suddenly, blocking one of his spells. It bounced off the protective shield that I just cast, sending it back at him. His feet slid on the soft dirt, trying to stop but, it was too late. My rebounded spell had sent him flying off his feet and onto the ground where he lied motionless.

I quickly glanced around me to see where my uncle was. My heart beat out of its chest. I watched the Dark Shadows surround my uncle as he fought them three-to-one. He stood in front of my aunt, protecting her from the looming danger as she lay asleep on the damp forest floor. Evelyn's dark-black hood flew off, exposing her face as she cast her curse, hitting my uncle directly in the heart.

I couldn't speak. I couldn't move. I watched as he slumped to the floor, his once bright green eyes now glassy and lifeless, staring up at the sky. Another Dark Shadow conjured the same curse and hit my aunt, her last breath leaving her smooth lips before her chest became motionless.

Their bodies lay still, side by side.

CHAPTER 20

Merissa

Tears seeped out of my eyes uncontrollably. I dropped to the ground, my body numb. All the shouts, from both the Dark Shadows and the Rebels, phased out, leaving only silence.

I couldn't believe it.

My body shook as the tears flowed out of me. Through my blurry vision I could see the two Dark Shadows that had murdered my aunt and uncle coming towards me; their wands raised in preparation for a fight. Evelyn stood in front of the two bodies, kicking them with her toe to make sure they were dead.

Rage like I had never felt before flooded through me. I could feel it coming, that feeling of overpowering energy spreading through every inch of my body. I screamed, letting it all out; the anger, the pain, all of it. The ring vibrated on my finger.

A wave of magic burst out of me as I casted. The two Dark Shadows, who were inches from me now, were hit with the blast. The magic swarmed their bodies and incinerated them where they stood, along with anyone else close to me.

I didn't care who got hurt. I wanted them all to feel my pain.

More Dark Shadows came running towards me, their wands raised to subdue me. With the flick of my wrist, they were flown through the air, landing hard in the mud. Others, who were on their way to help, ran in the opposite direction.

Within a few minutes, the area had been cleared, everyone in the vicinity was running for their lives.

I turned towards the bodies of my Aunt and Uncle, searching for Evelyn who had been blown a few feet away by my magic. She slowly crawled into a kneeling position, her eyes wide with shock.

I walked towards her, letting my magic crackle and blaze in my hands.

"Please! Don't..." she begged, her hands in front of her, surrendering.

But I continued forward, a ball of dark, malevolent magic in my hand.

"Merissa, I'm sorry! Please don't hurt me!" she pleaded, with tears of fear running down her face as she crawled away from me.

"You murdered them!" I shouted, flinging magic at her.

Screams echoed through the forest as my magic hit her square in the chest, making Evelyn crumble to the ground in pain. She clawed at the spot where the magic hit, ripping her clothes as she tried to make the pain stop. Dark lines began to grow on her skin, just as it had done with Athena, spreading all over her body.

I watched as Evelyn curled into a ball, crying and screaming in agony. Slowly, her breath slowed, and the screams stopped. She lay there on the forest floor, immobile, the black lines covering her entire body.

I crumbled to the ground beside my aunt and uncle, laying my head on my aunt's still chest as I cried. As I lay there, the anger I felt subsided, leaving me with an empty hole in my heart.

Killing the people who murdered them didn't help the pain. It only made it worse. It made me just as bad as they were. Aunt Lucy would never have wanted this for me, yet it happened.

All the energy I had was gone. I cried myself dry, leaving my swollen eyes sore. I lie there motionless, listening to the wind rustle the leaves on the trees and letting the soft drops of rain hit my face.

Was this what it was like to be dead—peaceful?

I wished I could go with them. I wished I could hold their hands one last time. I never got to say goodbye. But I knew that I couldn't give up now. They died to save me and I couldn't let their sacrifice go in vain.

I struggled to pull myself up, looking around for anyone to help me get to the meeting point. Silence spread through the forest. I was alone. I had driven everyone away.

I pulled myself to my feet, clutching a tree for support. Each step was a struggle, feeling like I had been walking for days, but I continued on through the forest.

In the distance, I could see the figure of a person. I slowly moved in their direction, hoping that they would lead me to the rest of my family.

As I got closer, I could make out the figure, a black cloak wrapped around him. Vince stood before me with Julia flanking his side.

"You're even more powerful than I thought possible, a witch who uses magic without a wand. Impressive. I must say, this had never been recorded before.," said Vince, a smirk crossing his face.

I used what strength I had to straighten my back, showing that I would not back down.

"It's a shame to lose Evelyn and Justin. Such devoted supporters they were...But we'll find others, once we have the power that you hold."

Chapter 21

Derik

I followed Jennifer and Herald down a steep, dark slope that hurdled into the ground. This seemed all too familiar. This hideout was the one that the vampires used previously before our position had become compromised and we had moved to the Underground.

My legs burned as I carefully descended the slope. The sky soon transitioned to dirt and rock as we slowly moved downwards. The overpowering smell of mold crept into my nose. Torches lit the path but the light was dimmed by the hundreds of people flooding through the tunnel.

Soon the slope evened out into a flat walkway and the hard walls of the tunnel spread wide as we entered the underground hideout.

Over the top of the pile of heads in front of me, I could make out the town. It seemed that the Rebels had only repaired half of it, while the other part seemed to continue to rot and wither with time. Large fire lit street lamps were placed along the walkways, allowing light to pass through the dark cave. Pieces of rotting wood and molding rock were moved to the edges of the cave, allowing easier movement across the area.

For a second, I felt homesick. I missed my mother and all the vampires I knew back in my version of the Underground. But, I shook those feeling aside. Throughout my journey, I had met many more people that I care about and they were now in immediate danger. My family was safe from the Dark Shadows as long as they stayed below the surface. Merissa was not safe anywhere she went. I had to focus on her.

As we went further into the town, I could make out Darius standing on a large podium, ordering people to find a structure to take refuge in.

"This way," Herald called as he led us to a small, single story wooden home.

He opened the door, peering in to see if it was already occupied, before entering. The small house had multiple bunk beds, just like the Rebels headquarters had, and a small kitchen on the other side of the house.

Jennifer stood at the open door, peering out.

"There's a tall ledge over there," she pointed, "I'm going to stand on it and hopefully find everyone else."

Harold nodded his head in approval before she left closing the door behind her.

. . .

It felt like hours had passed. I paced around the house anxiously while Herald sat by a window, staring out in search of his family.

"She's back," he called.

I immediately held the door open, waiting for Merissa and the rest of her family to join us. Jennifer and Emma entered the house with glum looks on their faces. I waited for Merissa to walk into the house. I peered around the door to see her but, she wasn't there.

"Where's Merissa?" I asked.

"We couldn't find her. The crowd is thinning out and there is still no sign of her. I think something is wrong," said Emma nervously.

"Did you see Ashtyn and Lucy? She was with them,"

asked Herald, a look of panic on his face.

"There was an attack at one of the tunnel exits. Did everyone make it back?" called Richard as he marched into the house, panicked.

Herald ran towards the door, swinging it open with a loud bang and rushing outside.

"The rest of you stay here. We're going to find our daughter," shouted Jennifer as she left for the surface.

I wasn't going to be left behind. I knew that I had to do something or else I feared that I would go insane waiting.

"I'm going with you," I shouted before dashing out of the door.

Chapter 22

I inched back, my weak legs shaking with every step. The Masters stood in front of me, their wands out in case I decided to flee. They would have to kill me if they wanted to get to my magic. I would go down fighting just as my aunt and uncle had. I was not running anymore.

I clenched my fists, conjuring my magic. I could feel the energy swirl inside of me, but this time I was in control. I took a deep breath, bracing for what was to come.

"Don't try it Merissa," said Vince, "There's two of us against one of you."

"That didn't stop me before, now did it?"

Vince aimed at me, uttering a sedation spell. As the spell sped towards me, I extended my arm calmly. The spell made contact with my hand, allowing me to grasp it. With shock spreading across the Masters faces, I crushed the spell, sending glittering dust like particles raining down to the ground.

"She's too powerful. Let's just get rid of her and take what we can from the body," said Julia, with fear in her voice.

"No! We need it all..."

"You want it all! She needs to be stopped before she ruins everything we have worked for. Kill her Vince!" yelled Julia.

A dark orb manifested at the tip of Julia's wand. I braced myself for the spell to hit me, my hand outstretched just as I had done previously. Before he could finish the spell someone hit him from behind tackling Julia to the ground a few feet away. Derik hunched over Julia, his hands wrapped around her throat. With a quick movement of his arms, a loud snap came from Julia's neck. Julia went limp, her neck bent in an odd position with a bone protruding through the skin.

Vince screeched at Derik as he turned his attention to him. Curses flew out of his wand. Derik easily averted them, leaping into the air and landing in a crouched position behind the lone Master. Out from behind the trees came my parents their wands raised and already firing spells towards Vince.

I tried to move away from the fight to get to safety and regain my strength while I could, but my shaking legs gave out making me fall to the ground. As my parents fought Vince, Derik ran to me. I could see fear in his eyes. Fear for my safety.

"I'm alright," I said in a shaky voice.

"The trees are denser up there. It will be harder for the Dark Shadows to take a shot at you. We need to go there now. Your parents will handle them until I get back to help."

He quickly lifted me to my feet. I put my arm around his shoulder for support as he carefully took me in the direction of the dense line of trees ahead of us.

"Wait," I shouted.

Vince's spell had made contact with my father's dueling hand, sending his wand falling to the ground. He yelled out in pain, his hand obviously broken. A curse formed at the tip of Vince's wand, ready to strike the killing blow.

Without hesitation, I conjured my magic and sent it flying at Vince. Time seemed to drag on for that moment slowing everything down. My spell hit Vince, absorbing itself into his body. A look of shock passed across his face. He stood frozen for a moment, unable to move. Then he collapsed to the ground, his glassy eyes wide open and unmoving.

The two Masters lay there, dead, their cruel reign finally broken.

I dropped to the ground, unable to speak. It was over.

Derik crouched beside me, holding me in his gentle arms. My mother ran over to me, hugging me on my other side and telling me that everything would be fine now.

I looked up at my father who was searching the forest.

"Where are Ashtyn and Lucy? They were with you right?" he asked.

I tried to speak, but no words would come out. I shook my head, unable to make eye contact. I could hear his rapid breathing and pictured a look of grief and despair cross his face.

My mother held onto me tighter. I could feel her wet tears slide onto my face.

"I'm so sorry, Dad," I sobbed, "I'm so sorry."

We sat there on the wet ground, holding each other in comfort for no words could explain the sadness that we felt.

CHAPTER 23

Merissa

I sat on a dusty wooden chair in the forgotten underground hideout, wringing my hands in my lap. The Masters were gone, yet it still didn't feel like we had won. Some Dark Shadows had fled after seeing my magic at its full strength. This left me with a sick feeling in my gut. They could always regroup and come back for me to finish what the Masters had started: to steal my magic and leave me for dead. It felt as if I would never be left alone. I would always be hunted for something that I was born with, something that I did not choose to have.

The loss I felt was even stronger than it had been before. I would never see my aunt and uncle again. The people who had raised me had died in order to protect me. Everyone else had made it to the hideout safely. It was only those who fought alongside me that were hurt.

Guilt ripped through me life a knife. I wished I could go back to that moment and redo everything. I could have stayed to fight alongside them. I could have used my magic to rid the Dark Shadows of this world long before they killed my aunt and uncle.

The nagging feeling of what I had done in my rage crept into my mind. I had taken several lives which was something that I thought I would never do. I didn't know who I was anymore. The events that had unfolded through the past weeks had changed me, but was if for the better or the worse. I really did not know.

I did what I had to do to survive. If I hadn't, Evelyn and all the other Dark Shadows would have continued to come after my magic and, eventually, they would have succeeded; I would be dead.

I lifted my head as I heard a knock on the door.

"Are you alright?" asked Derik.

I shook my head as he entered the room. He took a chair from the stack lined along the wall and placed it beside me, holding my hand in his.

"I know it hurts right now. In time that pain you feel will heal. I went through the same thing when my father died."

Tears welled up in my eyes. As one slid down my cheek, he caught it with his finger, wiping my face. He laid a soft kiss on my forehead, making me feel a moment of happiness.

"We'll get through this, together," said Derik.

I looked into Derik's eyes, knowing there was truth behind his words. Time will heal the scars that I had endured from the Dark Shadows. Even though it felt like I had lost everything, I have gained so much more. I found family that I didn't know existed and I found love.

The world was changing for the better because of me. The Dark Shadows were a threat no more. Although I had done some horrible things in order to get here, I will manage to forgive myself and move on. I am not a monster. I am someone who risked her life to make sure that no one would ever get hurt the way I did.

A sense of peace washed over me.

There is always hope for change. No matter how dark or how negative the world gets, I must always remember that happiness is just around the corner. I just have to wait, and it will come.

About Atmosphere Press

Atmosphere Press is an independent, full-service publisher for excellent books in all genres and for all audiences. Learn more about what we do at atmospherepress.com.

We encourage you to check out some of Atmosphere's latest releases, which are available at Amazon.com and via order from your local bookstore:

Heat in the Vegas Night, nonfiction by Jerry Reedy

Chimera in New Orleans, a novel by Lauren Savoie

The Neurosis of George Fairbanks, a novel by Jonathan Kumar

Blue Screen, a novel by Jim van de Erve

Evelio's Garden, nonfiction by Sandra Shaw Homer

Young Yogi and the Mind Monsters, an illustrated retelling of Patanjali by Sonja Radvila

Difficulty Swallowing, essays by Kym Cunningham

The Magpie and The Turtle, a picture book by Timothy Yeahquo

Come Kill Me!, short stories by Mackinley Greenlaw

The Unexpected Aneurysm of the Potato Blossom Queen, short stories by Garrett Socol

Gathered, a novel by Kurt Hansen

Interviews from the Last Days, sci-fi poetry by Christina Loraine

Unorthodoxy, a novel by Joshua A.H. Harris

The Alligator Wrestler: A Girls Can Do Anything Book, children's fiction by Carmen Petro

the oneness of Reality, poetry by Brock Mehler

The Clockwork Witch, a novel by McKenzie P. Odom

The Hole in the World, a novel by Brandann Hill-Mann

Frank, a novel by Gina DeNicola

My WILD First Day of School, a picture book by Dennis Mathew

Drop Dead Red, poetry by Elizabeth Carmer

Aging Without Grace, poetry by Sandra Fox Murphy

A User Guide to the Unconscious Mind, nonfiction by Tatiana Lukyanova

The Sky Belongs to the Dreamers, a picture book by J.P. Hostetler

I Will Love You Forever and Always, a picture book by Sarah Thomas Mariano

Shooting Stars: A Girls Can Do Anything Book, children's fiction by Carmen Petro

To the Next Step: Your Guide from High School and College to The Real World, nonfiction by Kyle Grappone

The George Stories, a novel by Christopher Gould

No Home Like a Raft, poetry by Martin Jon Porter

Mere Being, poetry by Barry D. Amis

The Traveler, a young adult novel by Jennifer Deaver

Breathing New Life: Finding Happiness after Tragedy, nonfiction by Bunny Leach

Oscar the Loveable Seagull, a picture book by Mark Johnson

Mandated Happiness, a novel by Clayton Tucker

The Third Door, a novel by Jim Williams

The Yoga of Strength, a novel by Andrew Marc Rowe

They are Almost Invisible, poetry by Elizabeth Carmer

Let the Little Birds Sing, a novel by Sandra Fox Murphy

Carpenters and Catapults: A Girls Can Do Anything Book, children's fiction by Carmen Petro

Spots Before Stripes, a novel by Jonathan Kumar

Auroras over Acadia, poetry by Paul Liebow

ABOUT THE AUTHOR

As an up and coming writer from Ontario, Canada, Brianna has a passion for spinning tales of adventure and fantasy. She enjoys taking readers on a ride through the realm of fiction by weaving magical and mystical stories that materialize from her wildly creative dreams and vivid imagination.

CPSIA information can be obtained
at www.ICGtesting.com
Printed in the USA
LVHW031910291019
635744LV00002B/2/P